David Stone lives pseudonymously in Johannesburg. *Too Deep Then* is his first novel.

TOO DEEP THEN

David Stone

PLUTO PRESS

First published in 1987 by Pluto Press
11–21 Northdown St., London N1 9BN

Phototypeset by AKM Associates (UK) Ltd
Ajmal House, Hayes Road, Southall, London
Printed in Great Britain by Cox & Wyman, Reading, Berks

British Library Cataloguing in Publication Data
Stone, David
   Too deep then. —— (Pluto crime)
   I. Title
   823[F]   PR9369.3.S/

ISBN 0 7453 0140 1 (pbk)
     0 7453 0136 3

CARA MONIA

The war drums rumble, the nation's generals grumble
and threatened by the black mass power politicians humble
While there round the bend where the dark meet the dead
and gutter bums lie 'neath the skyway
well you can't look away from dead dogs that lay
in the middle of the highway

The mist of the morning hides like a warning, the ghettoes
as guilty ghosts boast of patrols at every outpost
while dogs always bark at men that are dark
and deeply suspicious
does it come as a shock when you shiver in the stark
and night-time seems so vicious

> *Oh Cara Monia don't lie in bed with the blankets over your*
> *head*
> *Oh Cara Monia don't pretend to sleep when you're wide awake*
> *instead*

Forbidden men sigh, night-time calls its curfew
and dignity denied like a weapon backfires when misused
While the hidden trespassers and petty pass-law offenders
the accused confined, abused innocently surrender
but remember so well

The horror of tomorrow lies in young faces of the future
with fists in the air infants are aware of the creature
if it's shit that you sow, why shit you shall reap then
if you move too slow you'll find you're in it too deep then
amen amen amen

Oh Cara Monia well you're not to blame for the shape that the
world is in

Stan James

TOO DEEP THEN

FOREWORD

Do you remember 1974? There are two ways of remembering old times – either you remember what you were doing that year or you recall what was happening in the world outside.

I was born in 1952. My father was owner-director of Cummings Construction and was in those days very rich. Now, of course, Cummings has been taken over by a mining group. Dad has a seat on the board and is now very, very rich. He is, in the first instance, a coper – he coped well with having a daughter and never led me to believe he would have preferred a son. He is such a good coper that he does not appear again in my story.

Mum does, unfortunately. She is, forgive me Mum, a stupid woman – spoilt, flighty, slow to anger, obsessed with trivia. Everyone says I am just like her but I know that is not true.

In 1974 I was a fifth-year medical student. I lived alone in my own flat. I was 22 years old and had had six affairs.

I remember that I have always wanted to be a doctor but I can never recall for what reason. I often say it began when I was ten and a family friend of my father's asked what I was going to do when I was big. Did I want to be an engineer, a lawyer, a doctor? My mother replied, 'She can't be a doctor. She's a woman.' I think I decided then to do medicine.

This is the story I tell, anyway. In truth, I cannot even be sure it happened.

Van Wyk once told me that in the Soviet Union the vast majority of doctors are women and that this is logical because women more naturally have qualities of caring and compassion. In the past ten years I have swung back and forth across that statement: women do have more compassion; no, they do not; yes, they do; caring is a part of medicine; no, it is just hype put out to fool the public; the Soviet Union treats women equally; no, it does not; yes, it does, better than America anyway.

Van Wyk also said to me once that there are some things one should not try too hard to explain. That I believe, at any rate.

In 1974 the world had never heard of Soweto; hardly anyone knew of Frelimo or the little bearded man who was its leader.

In South Africa no one had heard of Neil Aggett; the emerging trade unions hadn't yet emerged; and surveys by newspapers still showed that a majority of Afrikaners would be willing to die to keep blacks out of rugby teams and bars.

In 1974, everyone prophesied enormous civil unrest in South Africa. Few thought it would be a daily occurrence, immutable, accepted like the sunrise.

Germaine Greer still believed that the sexual revolution would bring freedom to women.

They were dark and passionate times, those. That's where my story starts.

CHAPTER 1

I suppose you could say it all started with the sick Racist Capitalist Sexist South African Society and its Running Dogs. I mean not directly; but like the finger flicking over the first domino and all the rest following clackety-cantle, until suddenly all the pieces are face down and you can't really remember how they fell or what it was like before.

This particular Running Dog was Whittaker: Dr Whittaker, Fellow of the Royal College of Arseholes or something, I've no doubt. We were having a tutorial around the bed of an old black man who was a terminal alcoholic and, not surprisingly with Whittaker, we were talking about peripheral nerve injuries.

'And the last category is that of the hysteric.' I watched Allan begin to pick his nose. 'You can often spot the case of hysterical nerve lesion because of the unanatomical distribution of the sensation loss.' Allan claimed that the technique of nose-picking was the same as that of a vaginal examination – Jewish noses and women who had had children deserved two fingers.

'For example, if they claim sensation loss in the hand below the cuff, and do appear insensitive to pin-prick, you may be able to increase the area of alleged sensation loss by surreptitiously sliding the sleeve a little higher.' Allan flicked a snot-ball under the bed and looked as though he were trying to poke an eyeball out.

'This phenomenon is particularly common in women, es-pecially young women.' What?! 'Now, if we move on to the sign of flapping tremor, which this patient fortunately exhibits very well . . .' Of all the nerve! This really was intolerable.

'Um, Dr Whittaker,' I broke in, 'do you realize the bias implied in that last statement?'

'What? Oh, you mean about young women, Miss–um–Cummings?' He glanced at my breasts, they all do it, no matter what I wear. Ask them the time, they look at my breasts and then at their watches. The other five students had woken up and assumed faces ranging from weary impatience to a grinning look-what-she's-up-to-now. Allan had stopped picking his nose and was staring goggle-eyed. At times like this I'm sure he doesn't know what year this is.

'You're implying, I think, that women are more prone to hysteria, neurosis, hypochondria or just plain faking. I mean that really is just a reinforcement of sexual stereotyping.'

'All I'm saying is that empirically, empirically, Miss Cummings, I, and my colleagues, have seen more cases of hysterical sensation loss in women than men. Your argument is like arguing that to say more non-Europeans than Europeans suffer from malnutrition is to spread racist propaganda.' A slight smile, a glance round at the other males in the circle, saying: I mean this girl no harm, one day she'll grow up as we men do. I noticed that he referred to me as 'Miss' but called male students just by their surnames. I didn't think this was the time to mention it. 'How many of these "colleagues" of yours are men, Doctor, and more important, how many of them share your antiquated preconceptions about the foibles of women?' Too late I saw the steel glint in his eyes behind their windows, too late I saw the jaw muscles bunch. Whittaker hadn't always been a Royal Fellow; once he must have been sharp and ambitious.

'Miss Cummings, you are not only being illogical, but repetitive. We don't have the whole morning for this case and you're wasting the tut's time. If you have any criticism of the way I conduct these sessions, you are welcome to speak to me

4

privately after hours in my office. Just phone my secretary and make an appointment. Now let's press on. Rabinowitz, can you demonstrate for us a flapping tremor?'

I would have been completely cowed by all this except, just before he turned away from me, he glanced at my breasts; just a quick one, but I spotted it. Honestly, the man was incredible. I glowered at the rest of the group, trying to will one of them to say something in support of my cause, but all five chauvinists kept still. I sulked through the remainder of the tut.

'A commendable amount of solidarity you showed there, comrades,' I sneered over tea after the tut. 'A really fine show, chaps.' We sat in the tearoom set aside for medical students in the basement of Groote Schuaur Hospital. Around us the talk was of incubation periods and heart murmurs.

'Ah, come on, Carol,' said Raymond in his odd high-pitched voice. 'You can't blame us for that. The point is, in that situation Whittaker was being entirely right and consistent and you weren't. I mean we know he's a bigot, but you can't shit a tutor out for his snide smile and suggestive wink – you have to get him on his words or deeds.'

'I suppose I shouldn't blame you guys for the answering snide smiles you give him either.'

'Carol, stop trying to cloud the issue. So-called solidarity is a real load of shit if it means supporting you in an argument based on a premise which is totally specious.' Thus Martin, small and compact in his matching shirt and tie outfit.

'Ooh, you . . . you dildoes.' I grabbed my books and marched out.

I was so annoyed I went home right then, although it was only two in the afternoon. That Martin is a real viper. We used to lurk around quite a lot together. In fact I admit it: I had had a crush on Martin for nearly two years. Every time he looked at me, my knees turned to jelly. The trouble was that he knew it and abused me in the subtlest way by being alternately warm and cool towards me.

I went to see a Glenda Jackson film in the afternoon which was so good that by the time I came out I'd forgiven him (and the others) their disloyalty. Glenda Jackson is my own private hero – I admit that I have spent quite a lot of time (well not hours, but some time) in front of the mirror trying to mime her expressions and way of speaking. I came to the conclusion that her strength lies in her chin and the way her flesh puckers on it – the sort of gift you're either born with or not. And I'm not. So what? We're unalike in respects other than our chins, too. My body is short and well, not quite plump, but it's not petite really, either. My legs are a shade too thick from all that hockey at school. But I do have a waist (and a belly, I admit) and my bosom is substantial. My skin's very fine and my hair is good to the touch but rather a dull, light-brown colour. I look better without my clothes on, I've been told. I'm not even the prettiest girl in my class, and there are only six of us. The prettiest is a German girl from Namibia who drives a red sports car, and I swear has a handbag made of genuine Herero.

When I got home I found a message from Martin, very long and repetitive – obviously a form of apology – to the effect that I was due to present a patient at the tut on the next morning. Apparently the notice about it had been up for two days now, so only the end-stage paranoids could suspect that Whittaker had just engineered it. But I did, anyway. At first I decided to ignore it and not go to school for the rest of the week, but my childhood of brainwashed conscientiousness got the upper hand after supper, and I dashed off to the hospital.

In the ward I discovered that the patient I was to present had been discharged that afternoon. 'If we'd known you wanted him, we would have kept him another day or two,' the registrar assured me gallantly. Should I have been suspicious then? Did a shiver cross my spine? After all, if Whittaker hadn't pissed me off I would have begun the case in the morning, would have my original patient, and the Registrar wouldn't have said next: 'Try Mrs Arendse in the corner on the right. She's going to cardiac surgery tomorrow afternoon, beautiful murmurs, wonderful pathology. It's a miracle she's lived so long with it.'

'Won't being the centre of a tut upset her quite a bit?' I asked.

'Nah, it'll take her mind off the op. Go on now, she's superb. I'll give you a hint, listen to her heart with her lying on her left side.'

I went. I mean I was just looking for a quick, easy case; I didn't really want to consider the person involved. I suppose I was as bad as the Registrar – his morality had been quashed by years of insensitivity, mine too easily in the pursuit of the short cut . . .

I began to take a history from Mrs Arendse in the staccato fashion prescribed: the encapsulation of life into a series of questions with a small range of answers.

Full name? – Valerie Arendse.

How old are you? – 61.

Are you married? – My husband died ten years ago.

Where do you live? – In Lavender Hill.

What do you do? What work? – I'm working in the kitchen for a baas in Wynberg.

Have you had any children? – Eight children. My Rienet . . .

Are they all well? – Only one lives, Rienet.

I looked at her for the first time – prematurely old, lean and stringy from a lifetime of manual work: only four teeth in her mouth – in the front; eyes strangely green in the hopeless brown wrinkles; grey hair unkempt. The bed was still neat from the last tour of the nurses, and her yellow-brown hands lay on the coverlet like a child's.

What happened to the other children? – They died. Life is hard on the flats, you must know. I had two other pregnancies

7

that I miscarried. Now only Rienet lives somewhere . . . I must see her still, I must . . .

Yes, well, have you been in hospital before? – Nooit. I saw the doctor only when the child died . . . so many times . . . now only Rienet.

She seemed to be wandering, so I pressed on.

Has anyone near you had rheumatic fever, or TB? – Yes.

What? – Many people. I had TB when I was 40 and all my sisters had rheumatic fever. That's what my mother said. We never saw a doctor unless we were very sick.

What made you see a doctor? How did you first become ill? – About six months ago, when I couldn't hang out the washing without getting short of breath, the Madam drove me to the hospital . . .

And so on. I hurried through the history, and the Registrar arrived to help with the salient points of the examination. Mrs Arendse was still while we probed, banged, stared at, listened to and measured assorted parts of her, but seemed to drift off about the past as soon as our attention shifted off her body, repeating the name Reinet over and over.

'All right, Mrs Arendse, I think that's everything. Tomorrow morning we'll have a tutorial around the bed, it won't take long.'

'But, Doctor . . .'

'I'm not a doctor, I'm a student. My name is Carol.'

'But I'm going to have an operation tomorrow.'

'No, that's in the afternoon. We'll worry you only for about an hour in the morning.'

'Oh, Doctor, I know I'm going to die tomorrow, I know.' To my embarrassment she began to weep and then to pant from shortness of breath. I felt ashamed, I know I should have found another patient, but it was already eight-thirty and I . . . well, I just couldn't be bothered.

'Look Mrs Arendse, I know it's your first operation but it's only a splitting of the valve, I mean they do a few like that every week. Compared to a whole transplant which they do now, a valve-split is nothing, really. Please, Mrs Arendse, don't cry now, you're only making yourself short of breath again. There, there.' I patted her shoulder, awkwardly surprised at the sharpness of her bones. I cursed my gaucheness.

'Has your daughter Rienet been to see you?'

I was answered by a wail that reverberated in the curtained space around her bed. 'I don't know where she is, I must find her, my Rienet.' I rushed out to get the sleeping tablet, the administration of which had been delayed by my presence. When I returned, she was a little calmer, her face smoothed out, her green eyes not so full.

'Look,' she said and pulled out from her nightie a crucifix on a chain. It was about five centimetres in diameter – a little Jesus stretched out in a circle. The sculptor appeared to have had difficulty with the fine work so it appeared that Jesus was gazing upwards and smiling. 'Is it copper?'

'Yes, and here and here see, it's gold, it's a bit dirty. The laughing Jesus, it belonged to my mother's mother's mother's mother's . . . um, five of them. I'm the fifth one to wear it, and it must go to Rienet now, I'm dying tomorrow. Rienet, how will it find her?' She was getting drowsy now, more from her emotional draining than the sedative, I think.

'Listen, Mrs Arendse, I'll see you tomorrow, you must go to sleep now.' I embraced her awkwardly, placed a kiss on her drying cheek and began pulling the curtains back. It was the first time I'd kissed a patient. It was also the first time I'd kissed a black. Her eyes were wide open now, watching me as I fastened the curtains back. 'G'night, see you in the morning,' I said brightly, and fled her all-knowing stare.

Mrs Arendse gave me a smile the next morning that could be described, I supposed, as wan, while I prepared her for the tut.

'I slept well but I dreamed so. All the people I ever knew I

9

think, I saw last night . . .' I gentled her into position. When the others had seated themselves around the bed, I began going through the presentation as fast as I could. I usually make a point of referring to women as Ms but I knew it would sound bizarre in this instance.

It all went off well enough; we had a listen to her chest, the tutor wished her luck with her operation, and we rose to discuss the case in the Doctors' Office. Martin and I stayed behind a while to help her dress. Immediately she began the routine of the night before – how she was sure she was going to die, and how could she ever get the laughing Jesus to Reniet?

'Look, Mrs Arendse, I'm sure everything will go wonderfully this afternoon. I tell you what, I'll even come and watch the operation, how's that?' I don't know why I thought she might take comfort from the thought that I, a stranger, would be watching some other gowned stranger slicing her up, but she did. I was already beginning to regret my impulsiveness – there was a Bogart movie I had planned on seeing that afternoon.

'Take this, give it to Rienet. Make sure that she gets it.' She pushed the crucifix into my hand.

'Mrs Arendse, I couldn't. I tell you, you'll be able to give it to her yourself in a couple of days.'

'Mrs Arendse, Carol will keep the charm till after the operation,' chimed in Martin, 'and then give it back to you safe and sound.' This seemed to satisfy everyone, and we hurried back to the tut. The laughing Jesus, heavier than it looked, swung pleasantly between my breasts.

Well, I suppose it's easy to guess what happened next. In the theatre Mrs Arendse gave me a white-faced smile just before being anaesthetized and I pointed towards my chest to show where the Jesus was hidden by the theatre gown.

The operation was comparatively straightforward and went quickly. It was complicated, however, by her poor general condition. Four times she went into cardiac arrest, and four times the defibrillating machine restarted her heart. Each time I thought I was going to die, not she. Just as the worst seemed over, and the surgeon was closing the chest, she arrested for the fifth time, the machine didn't help, and ten minutes later she was pronounced dead.

I didn't want to make a fool of myself in the theatre, didn't want these pigs to exchange superior smiles over the weaknesses of women. I walked out slowly and purposefully, down the passage, everything looking white, drained of colour, dead, pushed open the door of the change-room and only then passed right out.

CHAPTER 2

'You'll just have to try and find the daughter. You let yourself in for it. Now you'll have to make an effort,' said Raymond morosely. 'But it could well prove impossible. People come and go on the flats and there's no telephone to be located in a convenient directory. She may even be dead or living in another city'.

'Ah, bullshit, man!' Allan had just blown some Durban Poison in the toilets and was a little less lethargic than usual. 'I mean, can you imagine it? For five generations they've been passing that little charm along. Look at it, it's got a little gold in it. How many times, in five lives, how many times have the children gone hungry, while Mom still kept a bit of gold around her neck? A bit of gold representing Jesus Christ not wailing, not whining in puzzlement at his downfall, not being stoical, or gentle or long-suffering or holy, but laughing, look at him, nailed up there and laughing at God in defiance. What kind of philosophy is passed from mother to child under the influence of old giggling Joe here? Don't you think they teach their kids that life is a big joke, that no one is king, that there's no one you need be in awe of? . . .'

'The line would have died out four generations back if that had been true,' broke in Martin.

Allan brushed it aside. 'It's true, I know it's true. Look Carol you've got to find this chick, you just gotta! It's her birthright.'

'If Carol had to worry about restoring people's birthrights, it could turn out to be quite a long job. But I agree with you, it's worth making the effort.'

'What do you know about her, Carol? Shit, just the little we spoke to her in the tut; I thought she was fantastic. She came over as a really strong person, someone who'd seen it all, nothing surprised her, nothing life threw at her could faze her.' When Allan finally did fix his swivelling attention on some idea, he never let a little thing like The Real Facts distract his flow of thought. In five minutes he might be claiming that she had had the eyes of a dagga smoker and that he'd seen her nip in to the toilet for a zol that morning.

'The thing is that whenever she tried to tell me something about her background or this Rienet, I shushed her up and asked how many pillows she slept on at night or how far she could walk without stopping, or some such rubbish. Other than the name Rienet, all I know about the girl is that she doesn't, didn't, stay with her mother in Lavender Hill. I suppose I could get Mrs Arendse's last address from the folder and go and speak to the others in the house. Maybe they're relatives who know the whole story.'

'That's it, Carey girl, you get on the trail. Oh . . . fuck it!' Allan had begun spinning the sugar pot around about half an hour previously and he had only just managed to knock it on the floor. 'Hey, you remember that programme on the radio years ago? "Missing Person's Bureau." They used to start exactly the way you have – no clues, just a tiny lead which soon fizzles out'. He kicked at the pile of sugar ineffectually. 'Leaves the agent baffled till he plays a hunch and solves the case thirty seconds before the Chrysler advert.'

'Ja, I remember it,' said Martin. 'There were lines in it like "You're not from the police are you?" and "I don't like it, Chief, it just smells fishy". The case always started out straightforward and got more improbable till it ended totally unexpectedly. Usually a little bizarre but poignant.'

13

The four of us giggled together companionably in the deserted tea room. I reached out to pour myself a fresh cup and noticed that my hand had a faint tremor. I held it up, bewildered. I was conscious of a sense of anticipation, faintly sexual even. My heart was thumping in my chest. It reminded me of waiting to go out on a date. This search was the most exciting thing to come my way at medical school for years.

I had stopped laughing and the three of them stopped too. They turned to gaze at me, and we listened to the hum of the hospital above us.

I copied Mrs Arendse's last address from her folder and, Allan having begged off to score some acid, the three of us set off that afternoon for Lavender Hill. Lavender Hill is to housing what instant coffee is to beans. It's a fairly small township consisting of maybe two dozen or so large three-storey tenements thrown up at any angle to each other. They are built of prefabricated cement walls, the outsides of which it is illegal to paint, decorate or in any way render different from the drab grey that the blocks were when they emerged from their moulds or whatever. There are no gardens, no pavements, no street lights, just roads of the coarse white sand that makes up the Cape Flats.

Lavender Hill was only two or three years old, but already it was falling apart. In fact the holes in the walls gave the impression that someone was kicking it apart. We found the block called Zonnekus and stopped the car outside. A crowd of locals of varying ages surrounded us and watched us blankly from a distance of several metres. 'Soek jy Gunston?' asked one urchin with squint eyes. To them any whites, particularly men with hair so long they couldn't possibly be policemen, must be looking for Dagga to buy when they came to the Hill.

We found the flat where Mrs Arendse had stayed, right in the corner on the top storey. The door was opened by a youngish man in his 30s, who looked in bewilderment from one to the other of us, his eyes wrinkled by hangover.

14

'Ya,' he said. For a moment I wished he were old enough still to be awed by white people.

'Um . . . we're looking for Mrs Arendse,' I broke in quickly before Martin or Raymond could speak. I didn't want them directing the show.

'She's dead, sorry,' he said, moving to shuffle back into the flat again. I hadn't had time to collect my thoughts.

'Well, we're actually looking for her daughter, Rienet.'

'She doesn't live here.'

'Look, we were with Mrs Arendse when she died and she asked, well begged us really, to see that her daughter got that charm she wore around her neck.' Martin smiled persuasively at him. How I hated him, he'd somehow managed to convert 'my' quest into 'ours'. And, anyway, what business did he have intervening, just because I was screwing up.

'Ja, but I never met her daughter, you know,' the surly one was brightening under the influence of Martin's charm. 'Tannie Arendse just used to board with us, she wasn't no relative or anything.'

'Couldn't you think of some way we could contact her, Rienet I mean?' I said.

'Listen, come back and see my wife when she gets home. Mrs Arendse came to us from District 6, y'know, when she was thrown out there. My wife might know who she stayed with, she gets back about seven.'

We trotted down the stairs and took the long road back to the town. We finished a bottle of wine at Raymond's house, made some tomato and onion sandwiches, and went off again, back to Lavender Hill. This time things went a little smoother. Lettie, Joe's wife, was a garrulous factory worker. 'I only get a chance to talk at home,' she said with a wink and laugh. 'The machines make too much noise.' In fact getting Lettie to talk was far easier than getting her to shut up again. Soon we had the whole story about Joe's drinking, his unemployment, his other women. She ignored Joe's scowls and muttered comments. She was just getting to his greedy sexual habits (was this the site of power in the house? was this the reason she didn't fear his threatening looks and calloused hands, because she could control the faucet between his legs?) when I interrupted, gaily but forcibly, and steered her round to Rienet and her mother.

'Yes, well, Tannie Arendse was always speaking about Rienet – that's all she ever spoke about, eh Joe? But I never heard how they got separated. Tannie Arendse used to stay in District 6 before she came here to us. Shame, she was such a good soul, and that chain with Jesus, she used to touch it all the time. Mind you, I didn't like it myself, I'm a Baptist. I always says you can believe what you like but don't mock God. Hey, Joe man, what about old Mrs Aries from next door, she came out the district as well. Hang on, Carol, I'll go see if she knows anything about Rienet.'

Lettie burst out and we were left staring at the yellow walls. Joe took the opportunity to ease himself out of the flat, probably to find something to drink. Children of assorted sizes careered round the place; but which were Lettie's and Joe's and which belonged to the other couple they shared the three rooms with, I had no idea.

Lettie returned flushed with triumph. 'The old cow doesn't remember Rienet but she says that Mrs Arendse used to stay upstairs in a house the corner of Hanover and Smit Streets.'

We thanked Lettie profusely, refused an offer of more tea (we only accepted the first for fear of causing a racial slight), and fled before she had time to notice that Joe was gone again.

Martin and I climbed out of the mini at the corner of Hanover and Smit Streets. There were no buildings there. In fact, there were no buildings for several blocks in every direction. The winter sun glinted on the weeds and grass growing out of the rubble. Little puddles had formed here and there from the rain the night before. I walked back and forth among the gravel plots, flicking stones aside with the point of my boot as though to uncover some hidden message.

Martin was leaning against the car, watching me with what must have been mounting impatience.

'For Christ's sake, there's nothing here. Let's go, Carol. There's no sense in spending the whole day here.'

'Oh, stop whining,' I snapped. I was, well not pleased, but grateful for two things. First, the enthusiasm of my three companions had diminished with each passing day – as borne out by the drop-out rate – while my own had increased correspondingly. And secondly, I knew with absolute certainty that my search hadn't ended yet. It was just a question of whether I'd be rid of Martin before or after the next 'clue' appeared.

I stopped pacing around and looked at the nearest buildings. The mountain was behind me, the sea in front. To my left, perhaps a kilometre away, the buildings of the city began to rise – first two storeys, then three, five and ten. To my right the white suburbs blossomed amongst parks and playing fields. And between these four landmarks we stood, in four or five square miles of gravel. Bizarrely, the streets criss-crossed as in any other suburb. Some of the plots were red-brown and still had pieces of buildings on them. Others, like ours, were green with vegetation, pointing to their devastation some months ago.

I walked back to the car. District 6 was the obvious direction for the city to grow in. And if blacks didn't share in the power structure, then obviously they had to be evicted and pushed out to the Flats. What surprised me was that there was to be no rebuilding until all traces of the old District had been destroyed. It was as though the destroyers deliberately wanted to heighten the dramatic effect.

'It's fantastic, isn't it?' said Martin. I flashed him a contemptuous look for stating the obvious.

17

We stopped at the first building we came to – a Malay-owned curry restaurant. We sat down and ordered small dishes of 'mild' curry and rice.

I walked over to the owner, a kindly old man with lots of smile wrinkles. 'We move to the city centre next week – a takeaway restaurant,' he said with distaste. He'd had the shop for twenty-five years. I told him my story. He remembered Mrs Aries well, and Mrs Arendse vaguely but not her daughter. 'Try the school,' he suggested, 'maybe they have records . . . If Rienet stayed here, she must have gone to the school, if only for a couple of years.'

We got directions and gulped down our food.

'That was super. Thanks Mr Agerdien, I'll come back again,' said Martin as we left.

'Better make it quick, they're pulling down the building next week,' said our host with a tired grin.

The headmaster of Walmer Estate School dressed with Afro style – if not length – hair. He was rather attractive; and rather unfriendly.

'. . . so I'm trying to find her daughter – it's almost my duty now,' I said with a little laugh. He had a stony face. 'Anyway you're just about my last chance,' – his eyebrows rose a fraction – 'to find her, I mean. Where else could I look?'

'Yes, ah, well even if she did come to my school in the last ten years I wouldn't be able to help you. I couldn't identify most of my pupils this year – there are over a thousand now – let alone any other year. We don't keep progress reports of our old pupils, you know.' His lips curled down a bit. He moved his eyes to a point two feet above my head. And stared.

'Please, isn't there anything you can do? Her name is Rienet Arendse . . .'

His eyes flicked down to mine. (They were grey. A black man with grey eyes!) Silence. 'No, I've never heard of her. Now you'll have to excuse me, I have reports to initial.' He stood up.

18

Not very tall, maybe two inches higher than me. 'And I'd advise you to find a crusade a bit more feasible and suitable for a white woman such as yourself.'

'Fuck you,' I said distinctly as I flounced through the door he had opened for me, 'Bourgeois Turd.'

'But he knows the name, I swear it. He almost flinched when I mentioned it.'

'Carol, I don't know what's come over you. You seem more out of contact with reality with each passing day.' It was teatime again and the four of us were sitting dunking Marie biscuits into lukewarm cups. There seemed a golden flush to the air. The boys' faces all seemed too close. I shook my head as though to clear it. Maybe Raymond was right, maybe I was cracking up. 'His answer was completely believable – I mean if he did know her amongst the thousands he has seen, that would be the strange phenomenon. Look, face facts. At the moment it seems impossible to trace the kid. It's unfortunate but there's no sense in making connections where none exist.'

'But you don't understand – in this business the unusual, the bizarre, is the commonplace. I mean this guy is a smoothie. Why should he be discouraging, almost to the point of rudeness, if he weren't covering up?'

'Carol, I can't believe it is you speaking, baby. Is this the same chick that told me last week that mind-expanding drugs were counter-revolutionary? All you feminists end up the same way, as mystics. Go to it, Carry, look for your Holy Grail. The search is the thing, remember.' Allan appeared to have more to say but had finally managed to cram three biscuits into his mouth at once. We watched him chew for a while, gurgling triumphantly.

'I refuse to be baited. I'll prove to you I'm right, and that's all there is to it.'

'Walmer Estate High. Mrs Reynolds speaking.'

19

'Good afternoon. This is Mrs Botha of Coloured Affairs Department. Is the Headmaster there?'

'No, I'm afraid Mr Van Wyk is coaching rugby this afternoon. Can I help? I'm the Vice Head.'

'Oh, I do hope so, Mrs Reynolds. We're producing a newsletter for coloured headmasters throughout the province and I'm just checking on their addresses. You don't happen to know Mr Van Wyk's, do you—?'

'Yes, it's, uh, um, 37 Chopin Road, Steenberg.'

'Thanks so much, Mrs Reynolds. We shall overcome! Bye now.'

So there I was at about seven-thirty that night, ringing the bell of number 37 Chopin Road. It was a neat, middle-class but not wealthy township. The houses were all the same design but had been decorated and painted according to various tastes (most of them bad, I thought). The door was opened by a stout elderly woman in an apron who did a double-take and then, more out of confusion than convention, showed me to a room at the back of the house where Van Wyk boarded. She knocked on the door and announced that he had a female visitor. He must have been expecting someone else (or had he been expecting me?) because he shouted to come in.

He was lying on the bed in his rugby togs. He stared at me for a few seconds, then motioned me to the only chair. I sighed with relief. At least he hadn't kicked me out.

'Of course, it was you that phoned this afternoon. You know, Mrs Reynolds draws a double cheque each month.' He was gazing at the ceiling again. 'One from CAD for teaching and one from BOSS for spying.' He shafted me with his grey eyes now. What a ham. But I was conscious of being pleased that by coincidence I was wearing a dress for a change – and no bra. I was also conscious of feeling a little guilty, because it was not really a coincidence. 'It would help if you were a little more careful in the future with whom you trade liberal slogans. My

20

position is open enough to compromise without your making it worse.'

'I'm very sorry. I didn't think.'

'It doesn't matter. But it strikes me I should remember that you probably quite often "don't think".'

'As you like. Why did you flinch when I mentioned Rienet Arendse's name before? I think you know more about her than you're letting on. I demand to know the truth.'

'You demand! You demand! You stand in my own room and make demands!' He was shouting, but I could see that he wasn't really cross. 'Just let's suppose, for argument's sake, that you're right and that I know something about this girl. Why should I tell you? What have you ever done for me? What are you ever likely to do for me?'

'But why not tell me?'

'Why not? My dear white princess, look outside this room, you'll see a thousand reasons, millions of reasons, why I should not respond to you with normal courtesy.'

'But what about Rienet? This is her property, she's entitled to it. The laughing Jesus would make her happy.'

'How typical of you whites to bring the notion of property into your arguments!' I coloured. This guy was sharp. 'In any case, I see this inheritance purely as a last attempt by a mother to make her daughter feel guilty for leaving home and remaining out of contact. No, unless you can offer me some incentive, I'll be forced to say that even if I did know anything of her, I wouldn't disclose it. To you.'

Pause. 'Money?' I ventured.

'Please, Mrs Botha, don't judge others according to your own ethical code.'

'My name is Carol Cummings, I told you before.' I saw by his smile that he hadn't forgotten. I certainly seemed to be losing the initiative. 'Well, what can I offer you, then?' I asked.

He cocked his head on one side and looked at me with

narrowed eyes. 'How much do you want to find Rienet? Is it a game for you, a diversion? Something to make you forget the emptiness of your life? A sop to an uneasy liberal conscience? A good yarn to impress your friends at the beach? What would you sacrifice to get what you want . . .?'

We stared at each other for a few seconds. Suddenly I stood up, turned on my heels and opened the door. As I stepped over the threshold, getting a good grip on the handle to slam it hard behind me, the crucifix bounced briefly against my breast, and I experienced an instant revelation. I suddenly understood what he meant. I was going about the search in a dilettante way with the same pink quasi-ideals I always had. It became important to me, as well as to him, that I should make some form of sacrifice, prove to us both that I was serious about the whole business.

I stepped back inside the room, closed it again and pulled my dress off over my head.

Van Wyk wasn't the least bit surprised. He smiled cock-surely to himself and stood up. Any thoughts we might have had about meeting naked dramatically in the middle of bed soon evaporated. Do you have any idea how long it takes to remove a fully laced pair of rugby boots? The initiative began to swing my way again . . .

As soon as it was over, while we were still panting – he more than I – I grabbed him by the hair and held his comb to his throat. 'Okay, buddy, what do you know about Rienet Arendse?' I said out the corner of my mouth.

'Nothing, Carol, baby, I told you,' he wheezed.

'What?'

'I remember her but I don't know a thing about her since she left school six years ago.'

'You shit! You dirty little liar. Why didn't you tell me?'

'I did, Carol, but you wouldn't listen.'

'You chocolate turd! I had to endure all that for bugger all!' I was dressing rapidly.

'Come back to bed,' he whined, making a playful grab for my rear. I whirled round and hit him as hard as I could on the temple with my elbow. 'You were a lousy fuck, anyway,' I said spitefully over my shoulder. This time I did slam the door.

CHAPTER 3

I went through the next few days as if in a mist. I went into medical school every morning for a couple of hours before retiring gracefully to roam around the grey buildings in town which housed the assorted South African bureaucracies.

Births and deaths were easy. I discovered, gratifyingly, that there was no record of her death. But there was also no record of her birth. I suppose that's not uncommon for her social group. I was making some progress with the Income Tax probe – a young clerk who had access to the files was going to take me roller-skating the next night. (Dammit, no! I was not going to sleep with him as well. To be suckered once was enough. Anyway, he had a bad dose of acne.) My own grip on reality seemed to be slipping a little, too. I couldn't seem to focus my eyes perfectly. People drifted in and out my vision, but almost half the time I focused just in front or just behind them. I was sleeping badly and had taken to drinking a couple of glasses of wine before bed in the evening.

On the third day after 'interviewing' Van Wyk, Allan took me aside after I'd served my two hours in purgatory for that morning.

'Gonna rush off now, Carol?'

I nodded.

'Listen, Carrie baby, I know it's none of my business, but you're looking kind of switched off lately. I mean you don't look at people when you talk to them – which is rare, which is rare –

and you've got these baggy things under your eyes. It looks as if you're smoking too much dope. Or is it love problems? Like I say, it's none of my beeswax, but if there's anything I can do . . .'

'It's none of your business,' I snapped, suddenly weary of his child-like persistence.

'Okay, Okay,' he said, all hurt, moving off. 'There's a letter for you. Been pinned on the notice board since yesterday.'

'Dear Carol [it began],

'Firstly let me offer my most heart-felt apologies. Thinking about it, I know you were right. I did deceive you about Rienet. But I like to think that I had a bit of help from you – I didn't have to work that hard in getting you into bed with me. For me, at any rate, it was a wonderful experience. I would very much like to see you again on any terms.

'As a token of my good faith, I'd like to tell you all I know of Rienet.

'Rienet was the kind of school-girl one gets every five years or so. They have an indescribable quality – a presence, charisma perhaps, impression of having seen it before. Rienet, when I last saw her, would have been about 13. I was teaching her general science that year, after doing history and geography with her the year before. She did not do outstandingly academically – used to come about fifth in class – but some subjects caught her attention and in those she did shine, in history for instance. Now, I do not know if you have seen the coloured (so-called) history syllabus, but it has a lot of guff about pluralism, separate development and cultural identity. At one stage the standard textbook even mentions the "traditional role of the black man as a labourer". Well, I was young and idealistic then and ran a sort of mini-civics course in history lessons. You know, the meaning of democracy and citizenship – liberal rubbish like that. Well, this I still cannot believe. Rienet was asking questions at the age of 13 that I laughed off – only to find myself returning to them three or four years later and realizing just how pertinent they were. They had overturned my whole liberal edifice in a couple of sentences; but I was too stupid even to notice.

'She also had a tendency to get into fist-fights and for her age I suppose she was the toughest kid in the school, male or female. I remember once she had a terrific fight with Amien Sonday who was fully two years older than her. I watched the whole thing from my office window. Rienet was smaller but very fast and strong, while Amien was a bull of a lad. Eventually Amien knocked her off her feet and put the boot in quite mercilessly. I could hear his feet thud into her ribs from my office and I only just managed to keep myself from running down to put a stop to it. Rienet was away from school for two days after that, but she arrived back wearing a big bandage round her chest and a tight smile. Anyway, six months later, Amien (whose father owns a shop) arrived on a spanking new Honda 50. Amien was so proud of it he couldn't talk (not that he spoke very much anyway). Two days later the bike was mysteriously burnt to cinders outside the school.

'Many people, including Amien who threatened to slice her up, thought that Rienet had been responsible. But she just smiled and cursed them all.

'The last time I saw Rienet was two days before school started five years ago. She waited for me at my car. She told me that she could not afford to come to school anymore; she had to find a job. She thanked me for my lessons, some of which she found "quite interesting" – those were her words. She had a strange, direct way of speaking to what most people would consider her superiors – she did not defer in the slightest. Anyway, I was so taken with her that I tried to persuade her to stay on – even offered her financial assistance. Of course she refused.

'And that's just about all I know of her. Except that she had a close friend at school called Didee. I have located her address (not without some trouble). If you would like to, we could both go round and see her.

Love,
Chocolate Turd Van Wyk.

So now there were two of us once more. But I felt much safer with Van Wyk than alone, or with Martin and the others – partly because he was black, but more because he radiated a kind of self-confidence that my puerile colleagues lacked. So, more contented than I had been for many days, we set off the next evening.

'Didee has married well, an up-and-coming accountant. I met him once socially; can't remember his name; a really bourgeois turd.' Van Wyk's eyes crinkled briefly as he shuffled through the gears in his old VW Kombi. We were heading out to Bellville South, a suburb of the coloured nouveaux riches.

'Tell me, why didn't you stop the fight Rienet was in? I mean if she were being so badly beaten . . . a man with your macho . . .'

'Well, obviously it wouldn't have made any difference. They could have just started again later. And I believe that fights should run their course. Rienet wasn't seriously damaged by it – neither her body nor her reputation. Also, there's a lot of knife-play at my school. I could just end up with a knife in my ribs for interfering.'

'I'm surprised you didn't give them boxing gloves and let them settle the thing man-to-man in the gymnasium like they do at military academies.'

Van Wyk's grey eyes twinkled. 'The analogy is not a bad one. Townships are very much like military colleges. Kids are taught, besides the academic stuff, to look after themselves, when to advance and when to retreat. Just as in an army, violence is always on the cards. They learn, too, that when there's a war on, they must move with speed and absolute ruthlessness.' He began to stroke my thigh through my jeans. 'Yes, I like that. A military college preparing the soldiers and the leaders for the coming war – the class war.'

'Sometimes you're really corny, Chocolate.' I removed his hand from my thigh. 'You haven't earned it yet this evening. In fact, I think I built up a fairly large credit last time I saw you.'

'Carol, don't be so single-minded. I thought we were friends as well.'

'Friends? I've only just met you!' We both began to giggle quietly, and I suddenly felt very close to him. Friends – just as he had said.

'Were you sexually attracted to Rienet?'

'Jealous?'

'Not even remotely.'

'In a way I suppose I was. She was a pretty girl, an early developer, she had breasts when she was 12. She was very fair – not that I go for whites as a rule,' he hurried on. 'But she had freckles and big eyes. She was small but very muscular. But it was her head more than her appearance that turned me on. As I mentioned, I used to run this mini-course in history – it might surprise you to learn that I used to be a flabby liberal . . .'

'Not surprised at all, actually.'

'Well, one day Rienet stands up and asks me "if citizens are those who have the vote, where does being poor come from?" Think about that. I have, a lot, over the past years. For me it encapsulates the limitations of bourgeoisie democracy. If the aim of having the vote is to gain control of a community's collective future, then why don't people who have the whole vote improve their own economic positions?'

'Well, don't they? Hasn't the lot of the working class in

Europe improved dramatically over the past century, with full suffrage?'

'Has it? I don't think so. I think the whole system has merely been stream-lined, which includes, oh, providing essential services like health so that the workers can reproduce themselves, education so that they can increase their own productivity, and fobbing off their political ambitions with a whole echelon of bureaucratized trade union leaders.'

'Aren't you speaking rather frankly in front of a white lady such as myself?'

'Perhaps, but now we are more intimate than most. Linked, one might say, by a stream of sperm from my reproductive organs into yours.'

'Oh wow! You are conceited.'

'We're here. Let me do the talking.'

'Why? You think I can't talk!'

'Another sherry, Carol?'

'Thanks, Arthur.'

Arthur poured an immaculate sherry with an immaculate brown hand coming out of an immaculate cuff-linked white shirt. Van Wyk sipped his beer with the air of someone who wasn't letting his contempt show. Didee blinked her eyes rapidly.

'Ja, Carol, I'm sorry I can't help you more. The last I saw Rienet, it would have been two years ago. You know, when she dropped out of school we always had to strain to see each other, until finally we only just bumped into each other from time to time. Also we were, how shall I put it, the same at school but once we left, we began moving very fast from where we had been – in different directions.' Didee shot Arthur an adoring look, arching her non-existent eyebrows. She relaxed back in her plastic foam easy chair and lit a long mild cigarette.

'What was she like, when you knew her well?'

'Well . . . she was very tough, you know? And . . . we sort of complemented each other. She would protect me physically when necessary and I would sometimes play up to being a child, helpless, you know. Like just before she left school she, well both of us really, we were very into shoplifting – and very successful we were too.' She giggled and glanced again at Arthur who grinned back tolerantly. She puffed on her cigarette and I noticed that she left a bright red stain on the filter. 'And one day we were caught. Twice. Well, the first time we scaled a jersey which I had put on under my blouse. This store detective, a big Boer with no hair, came and accused us. I don't know what made him wise to us; maybe he was just good at his job.'

'Probably a cabinet minister by now,' mused Van Wyk irrelevantly.

'So I really turned on the waterworks and told the manager how we didn't have money, and how my elder sister with me begged me not to for the sake of my syphilitic mother . . .'

'Syphilitic?'

'Well, I wasn't too sure what the word meant then. Eventually the manager let us go.'

'He obviously had a facile view of coloured diseases,' said Arthur.

'Then Rienet says: hell, no, we've got to get something else or we lose our nerve. You're crazy, I tell her. No, she says, adamant like, we've got to or we'll never do it again. So we go into a photographic shop and she shifts a camera – R39.95, I still remember the price – into her satchel. Now, I suppose it was a stupid enough move. I mean how many kids, let alone black kids, who don't look too rich, browse around a camera shop? So again we get busted. Let's see inside that bag, says this shop assistant. What, this one? asks Rienet, and she half opens it. As he bends down to get a good look inside, I see Rienet arching her neck as though she were gazing at the ceiling. Then wham! She butts him in the face, grabs my hand and we're running like hell.

Rienet sold the camera afterwards for R12 so that we each got R6.'

Van Wyk found that story pretty funny. He laughed uproariously and incited smiles from the rest of us. Five minutes later he was still chuckling.

'We always talked about getting out of the slums, you know. We used to fantasize, you know the way young girls are, about who we'd marry and what they'd do. Well,' a shrug of her shoulder and slight pout of her big red lips, 'I made it out of that shit hole, 'scuse language, and I only hope Rienet did, too.'

There was a long pause after that.

'Another beer, Ernest?' asked Arthur.

'Ernest? Your name's Ernest?' I asked Chocolate incredulously.

'Well, yes, actually it is. You mean we've been sleeping together all these weeks and you never knew my name?' I flushed while the others laughed.

'Get you back later!' I muttered. 'What has Rienet been doing since school, as far as you know?' I asked.

'She worked for Topstyle, the clothing factory, for a couple of years. Then, when she left, I hardly saw her. She was living with some not-nice type. Ferdie Martens was his name; he used to hang around the Kraal nightclub in Claremont. I don't know if she was working at that time. Oh yes, before that she had a scene with Armien Sonday.'

'I didn't know that,' exclaimed Chocolate.

'Ja, you know he was also at the school. You remember, um . . . Ernest, he and her used to be bitter enemies.'

'Then what happened between them?'

'Well, nothing, they just kind of petered out.'

'He was from a fairly wealthy family, at any rate,' contributed Van Wyk.

Didee rose to get a cigarette, revealing a surprisingly large bottom for someone who took such good care of her appearance.

31

'Rienet wasn't no gold-digger. Nor was I,' she added, in the pause that followed.

'No,' said Van Wyk, and no one knew what he meant.

'A successful evening, yes?' exclaimed Van Wyk, trying to squeeze my breast with his left hand while steering with his right.

'What was successful about it?' I said, leaning forward and parrying his hand off my shoulder.

'Three contacts that can be made – Ferdie Martens at the Kraal, Amien Sonday, and Topstyle. Also, we've traced Rienet's movements to only two years ago. What're you so depressed about?'

'I don't know really. But, from what Rienet seems like . . . what would she do with the laughing Jesus anyway? Melt it down for 75 cents? Pose as the Virgin Mary? Start her own church as a business concern?'

'Let's see it again, Ahh . . .' Van Wyk slid his hand up my jersey and grabbed the pendant in his fist, bumping his hand first against one breast and then the other. I felt too tired to stop him. Besides it was nice.

'You know what your problem is, Carol? You're disappointed that we're getting close to her. What'll you do when we find her? Go back to being a full-time, eager, ambitious young medical student? Stick your lights in strangers' eyes, your finger up their bums? What a bring down.'

'Spare me the cheap-jack psychologizing, Chocolate. You'd do better probing your own motives for being my Sancho Panza.'

'Well that's easy. I want you.'

'To sleep with me. No doubt you're still smarting about being called a lousy lay. I suppose you fantasize about me lying back completely sated, saying adoringly, "Ernest you're the greatest I ever had?" '

'You're very prickly tonight. Or some of you anyway.' He had slipped his hand inside my bra and was rubbing his palm against an indolent nipple. 'No, I really like you. Not your body or your sexual habits. But you. I like your style.'

'Corny, Chocolate Turd. All you want is to fuck.'

'Don't you?'

'Not particularly tonight, thank you.' I removed his hand firmly. My breast felt suddenly lonely and cold without him. I regretted my rash act, but I couldn't heal the breach between us without his jumping to the conclusion that I was available that night. I let it ride, and we sat in silence the rest of the way.

'So,' he said, as we pulled up to where my car was parked. 'Do you want to see me again?'

'Look, Chocolate, I'm sorry, I'm just a bit tense. I'm not sure how I feel about you. I don't . . . I don't usually go to bed with people out of gratitude or to prove points. I don't want to go to bed with you until I've worked out in my own mind what's going on.'

'. . . Sure.'

We slid into each other's arms and kissed for a while almost without passion, our tongues tickling necks and underlips.

'I noticed your friends tonight referred to themselves as blacks.'

'Umm. It just shows the pitfalls of Black Consciousness. Under no circumstances, whatever the forseeable economic phenomena, can Arthur and Didee play a role in the revolutionary process. Yet because they've a dusky skin, they're part of US against THEM.'

'Or, in my case, part of THEM versus US.'

'There you are, it just shows you how absurd the whole premise is.'

'But black consciousness has played a part in reducing the psychological effects of oppression, don't you think?'

'Possibly; but then it had no place adopting political

pretensions if it was a psychological weapon. And come to think of it, what's so great about it as a psychological tool? Wouldn't Worker Consciousness have done just as well?' Van Wyk had almost forgotten me now. He had his chin lifted, one finger raised for emphasis. At times it was difficult to remember he taught for a living; at others, like now, he clearly could be nothing else but a teacher. 'A movement dedicated to raising the people's consciousness of being workers – their long history, their formation as a class, their political destiny as foreseen by Marx; their need to assert themselves as workers when confronted by capitalists or labour aristocrats or, most of all, petty bourgeois opportunists, like Arthur and Didee.'

'Chocolate, you're sounding more and more doctrinaire the longer we associate. Haven't you heard? The ANC and SA Communist Party are calling for a war of liberation encompassing all progressive elements in the struggle. What's this ultra-left stuff you're talking?'

'Don't tease me about important matters. That just reflects the petty bourgeois nature of the leadership of those bodies. The workers are too militant to tolerate any of that two-stage theory of revolution. The Revolution is Permanent, and once it happens, it'll go on and on, smashing every organ and vestige of the capitalist state.'

'I've got you now, Chocolate. You're a fucking Trotskyite!'

'Yes, and proud of it.' I opened the door to get out. He leaned across, and I thought he was going to kiss me good night. Instead he hissed: 'We must return to the Classics – to works by Marx, Lenin and Trotsky. We must have our principles simply fixed in our minds – no matter what tactics we might adopt for the sake of expediency.'

'Goodnight,' I said, bewildered but still amused. 'Come around tomorrow night.'

CHAPTER 4

The next day I started work again, bright and early. I knew it would have been easier to work with Van Wyk but I felt, again, disinclined to share my obsession. Also, I was interested to see what kind of men Rienet went for. It was strange. I knew so little of her, yet I had a clear picture of her in my mind. I was playing a game quite often now. Well, it had begun as a game, but there had developed in the process an element of compulsion. I imagined what Rienet would do in my everyday situations. As I rode out to Elsies River, a traffic cop pulled up alongside me and gave me what he imagined to be a cool calculating look. I stared back. We stopped together at a traffic light.

'Can I buy you a coffee?' he asked, trying to be insolent and wheedling at the same time. His sweat, preserved as vapours by the chill air, bounced off my cheeks. I closed my eyes in disgust and was suddenly transformed into Rienet.

'Go fuck your mother's hand,' I said in Afrikaans (it sounds better in Afrikaans, fruity almost) and accelerated away, chuckling in triumph as I imagined Rienet would.

Sonday's Bazaars had recently been modernized into a small supermarket. Up in his semi-enclosed office, I introduced myself to Amien Sonday, son and heir. On first sight I was disappointed in Rienet. Balding and paunching very slightly, Amien was tall with straight black hair and a full Joe Stalin moustache. On his right hand he wore two big rings. He looked what he was: class bully turned businessman. Probably the two vocations were not separated by much, some might think (I know Van Wyk would).

'Let me get this straight now. You're looking for Rienet – going to all this trouble – to give her a charm that belonged to her late mother?' He spoke very fast. I felt suddenly embarrassed by the apparent stupidity of my quest. But how could I explain the importance to a stranger, even if he had been touched by the elusive Rienet.

'Not only that. Also to tell her that her mother's dead. Her mother attached a lot of importance to the . . . uh, crucifix.' I fingered it, feeling comforted.

'Maybe her mother attached importance to Rienet and not the charm, hey? Anyway I haven't seen Rienet for ages. We were . . . close for only a short while, a few months. Look I'll ask around and if I hear anything about her I'll phone you.'

Strike one.

As I drove out to Topstyle in Woodstock, I pondered on what the abrupt shopkeeper had said. It had been Martin who had suggested that I keep the Jesus while Mrs Arendse went to her operation. And possibly she had been using it as a reason for explaining to us why it was so important that she see Rienet – as if she needed an excuse for wanting to see her before she died. But that was quite irrelevant now. I was looking for Rienet, not to fulfil her mother's last request (had she even made one? It seemed so long ago I could hardly remember, though it'd been only slightly over two weeks), but for my own sake. No one who had been in contact with her had remained the same, except perhaps Amien, but I didn't know one way or the other about that. What could she do for me? Perhaps she had the answers to some questions I hadn't even worked out yet. In any case, I said to myself firmly, at least all this is something to do. I thought again of Van Wyk's diagnosis on the first afternoon we met: 'a white lady such as yourself'. I felt a sudden rush of warmth for him. He'd been right in his summing up of me, as he'd been right about most things.

I spoke to the receptionist at Topstyle who referred me to the second-floor foreman who referred me to the assistant director who referred me to the third-floor foreman who told me that he was not allowed to divulge worker information. 'You from the University?' he said suspiciously. While walking down the passage I was suddenly transformed into Rienet and thus disguised I burst into the personnel manager's office and told him my story. He was quite charming and we headed up to the fourth floor.

'It'd surprise you to know how few girls there are who've been here two years. Turnover is very high. This is the big problem for management. That and absenteeism. Still, I suppose it's understandable in view of the poor wages. Who can blame the workers if they are not very loyal?' he said, with a shake of his head.

Not I, I thought. And I'm also unimpressed by your attempt, Mr Personnel Manager, to take the workers' side. You are as clearly a part of the management as Mr Topstyle. I was pleased with the insight and reminded myself to tell Van Wyk about it that night.

We entered the fourth floor and walked along lines of impish young women chattering away at their odd-looking sewing machines. We made our way to one side of the floor where I was introduced to a Mrs Isaacs, a tired-looking woman in her late 30s. She was busy folding suits into boxes: a soft job as a perk for long service? She was uncommunicative, to say the least. Yes, she knew Rienet Arendse. Rienet had left the factory some two years before. No, she didn't know where she was now. I decided that I should leave her detailed interrogation for another day, when the smart-arse personnel manager was somewhere else. I thanked everybody profusely for their trouble and hurried off to my next port of call.

Strike two, I thought.

I walked up the stairs of the Kraal Nightclub, now conspicuously deserted in the daylight. I hoped this Ferdie character was around during the day. I didn't really fancy the idea of coming back at night, though I suppose I could have brought Van Wyk. Two young louts were hanging round the closed door at the top of the stairs. They eyed me in an overtly sexual way. 'Hey, hey goose!' called one. 'Howsit?' I said in what I imagined was a winning fashion. 'Make a pipe!' called the other, as I came abreast of them (I think they would have used a similar phrase from the way they were eyeballing my person).

'Actually, I'd rather make a Ferdie Martens,' I said. 'Do you know where I can find him?'

'You're lucky you approached me, like, goose, because I am just the man to put you in touch with Ferdie.' He leaned close to me, and I smelt that he had already made a pipe that afternoon. 'Our assistant manager,' he confided conspiratorially, and they both exploded with mirth in what was obviously a very 'in' joke. The ugly one opened the door for me, stood aside as I went in, nearly put his hand on my backside, then thought better of it (or lost his nerve more likely).

He showed me to a pokey office at the back of the club. 'Just hang on, I'll find Ferdie,' he leered at me. I sat down, feeling apprehensive at the frankly sexual vibrations in the air. I mean, if they locked the door, no one would ever hear what was going on inside this room . . . The door swung open, and I jumped. A short, thin man walked in, limping slightly. 'I'm Ferdie,' he said slowly, fixing his eyes on the floor. Oh God, Rienet, I thought, did you really have an affair with this rodent? I took a deep breath.

'Hello, I'm Carol Cummings. I'm a medical student at Groote Schuur. I became acquainted with Rienet Arendse's mother just before she died and she begged me to give this crucifix,' I showed it to him, 'to Rienet whom she hadn't seen for quite a time. I eventually got your name and I wondered if you'd know where she is.'

Ferdie lowered himself into a chair behind the door. 'Oh,' he said. Then suddenly, 'Who gave you my name?' and he raised his eyes to my chin.

'Didee, um, I've forgotten her other name – she's married to a lawyer.'

'That snooty bitch, yes', he said, nodding slowly as if that confirmed his suspicions. 'Uh, I haven't seen Rienet for a long time now. I don't think I can help you much.' He fixed his eyes over my left shoulder.

'Well, I've spoken to quite a few people about her now and she's . . . emerged as a very fascinating person. I'd be grateful if you could tell me what you know of her – some of what you know,' I corrected.

'She was great in bed,' chipped in one of the two goons who had sidled into the room behind Ferdie.

'Jasper, instead of talking kak about what you don't know about, why don't you do something useful like making us a pipe while we mull this issue over?' Ferdie looked full at Jasper but his voice was still soft and slow. Jasper slunk out chastened. They didn't laugh at Ferdie to his face at any rate, I thought. Possibly there's more to him than meets the eye.

'You do smoke it up don't you? Great. Tell me who you've seen so far.'

So I told him of my little odyssey up to that date, and he nodded as I introduced each new character. Jasper returned with a small sack and the neck of a mineral bottle. He put a whorl of silver paper in the mouth and filled the neck with dagga from the sack. 'Want to bust it?' he offered.

'No, you do it,' I said.

He lit up as Ferdie went on. 'As I said, I haven't seen Rienet for a long time, two years maybe. But Rienet was an important thing to me. In some ways she changed my . . . ta.'

39

He accepted the pipe and held it in both fists, sucking in hugely with his head drooped back. I watched incredulously as Jasper now exhaled an enormous amount of smoke – from mouth, nose and, good God, from his left ear! I took the pipe from Ferdie as he blew out no less a cloud. I held the warm bottle neck in one hand between index finger and thumb and sucked on it as confidently as I could, conscious that they were both staring at me. I held the smoke down and passed the bottle on. I could feel the tips of my fingers tingling as I exhaled slowly.

'Good stuff,' I said, feeling glad I was sitting down.

'From the Transkei,' said Ferdie diffidently. 'So tell me, Carol, why are you trying so hard to find Rienet? I know you promised her mother, but that thing round your neck is not that important. If you can't find her, you can't find her, you know what I mean?'

'It's just that . . . Rienet seems such a fascinating person from the way people have described her that I have to meet her. She seems so like the kind of woman I've always wanted to be.' Ferdie was nodding again. I wondered how coherent I was being. I was feeling decidedly odd. What's this? My turn again already? I sucked on it with less ardour.

'She was a looker all right,' put in Jasper as I handed him the pipe. 'No offence, Ferd,' he said in reply to Ferdie's solemn look.

'Jasper's got a perforated eardrum!' I sang out as I realized how he managed that trick.

'Bright medical student, hey?' said Jasper with a sneer. 'How about fixing Ferdie's leg then?'

'Did you hurt it?' I asked stupidly, remembering his limping gait.

'Wish I had,' he said expressionlessly. 'I had polio.'

'Oh,' I said biting back the reflex, I'm sorry.'

'So it's not a matter of just handing over the crucifix; you actually want to meet her face to face?' Ferdie passed the pipe.

'Yes' – drag – 'if possible' – drag. Over to Jasper.

'Inhale it through your earhole.' I was annoyed at Jasper's frivolous cruelty to Ferdie who was looking definitely more attractive now – hazier, but more attractive. And as I thought this, I realized that Ferdie and I were making eye contact. His eyes, like his face, held no expression. But they were quite, quite chilling. I looked away.

'Well,' he said, 'though I've no idea where Rienet is now, I've a lot of connections in the townships and I'll ask around. Leave your phone number, and I'll ring you if I hear anything.' He passed the pipe over. The room's dimensions had altered now – it looked very big, whereas before it had been quite small.

'Thank you. It's very kind of you to go to all this trouble,' I burbled.

'Think nothing of it. We're only the sea in which the fishes swim.'

'Oh, it's finished. Well anyway I must go. Thanks again.'

'Come again, goose, preferably without any pants.'

'Jasper, you're being a very irritating fucker today. If you don't come right soon, I'm going to tear your ears off.'

'Ah Jeez, Ferd, I was only joking.' And as I tottered out, I know beyond doubt, in that way you know things, really know them, without knowing why, that Ferdie was a killer.

Strike three (and was I out!)

I could drive all right. The reflexes were all there. But as I got to the end of the side-road from the Kraal, it dawned on me that I had no idea which way to go. I stopped the car and rested my forehead on the steering wheel, gulping air. Yes, now, town was in that direction, which was where I wanted to go, because Topstyle was on the way. I restarted the car, marvelling at my control of clutch and accelerator. I drove slowly with the window open, fancying I could feel myself sobering up. I arrived at Topstyle just on five as the crowd of working girls came spilling out. I searched frantically for Mrs Isaacs, wondering if I would recognize her. At last I saw her with a group of three younger women.

'Mrs Isaacs? Can I give you a lift?'

'I'm going to Manenberg.'

'Sure, I just want to talk to you without that personnel man around.'

'And my fren's?'

'Sure.'

We set off – a rather subdued lot. I scrambled my thoughts together. 'Why are you looking for Rienet?' asked one of the youngsters. I gave them the story, wondering how many more times I'd have to tell it. I hoped it would ease their minds about confiding in me.

'Why did Rienet leave?'

'She . . . was fired.' I raised my eyebrows. Mrs Isaacs went on reluctantly, 'I dunno if you remember, about two years ago we had a strike at Topstyle. We had two demands. One, a 15 per cent increase in the wages, and two, a creche for children. Many workers have young children, you know, it is a big problem for us. Well, Rienet wasn't scared of anybody, and as the strike went on she came to have more and more to say at the meetings. She kind of led the group of cutters who were very militant. The "cut-throats" they used to call us. The rest of us had babies, and it was the creche we wanted more than anything else.'

'Rienet doesn't have a child, does she?'

'Oh no. But she felt with us. Well, finally the bosses made an offer of six per cent with no creche and said it was their final offer. If we didn't come to work we'd lose our jobs. So in the last meeting – oh, I remember it so well,' Mrs Isaacs was growing positively animated, ' – the workers were split into the six percenters and the creche. Rienet said the bosses were bluffing. They couldn't close the factory down, and if they hired anybody else we could stop them from working. The arguments

42

went back and forth until Rienet suggested we should occupy the factory and live there until they gave in. Well, at that the six percenters took fright and forced a vote. They won, by a small majority, for going back to work. But that was with the men voting with them. Rienet wasn't satisfied. She shouted, how could the men decide to accept no creche when it was the women who had to look after the kids? The majority is shit, she said, and we took up the chant. She said the minority would be enough to occupy the factory. But now lots of the minority became afraid, and when another vote was taken whether to sit in or not we lost. The next day everyone was back at work, but at the end of the week Rienet was paid off.'

'How could they do that? Didn't the workers protest?'

'No, we didn't really. I suppose we'd just suffered a big defeat, and no one felt like fighting any more. We did send a deputation to the bosses asking that Rienet be given her job back, but then just after there was the fire, and most of us were laid off for two weeks while the factory was repaired.'

'A fire?' I repeated, my mind racing. I remembered the Honda 50 of Amien Sonday also consumed by fire.

'Yes, no one knows how it started.' Mrs Isaacs looked uncomfortable. Clearly the same thoughts had crossed her mind. 'No one was to blame; probably an electrical fault or something.' We had turned into Manenberg. The lights were on in the streets, those huge clusters of spotlights every few blocks set, vandal proof, at four-storey height.

'And Rienet? When last did you see her?'

'I've seen her only once since she was fired. I bumped into her about five months later in Athlone.'

'Where was she working then?'

'You know I didn't even ask. She talked on, wanting to know about Topstyle and what was happening, and were the cutters still together? and what about the creche?'

'Did you get the creche?'

'Yes, it started last month.' Mrs Isaacs gave a little smile.
'My children are at school now, the youngest of them.'

'Where was Rienet staying then, while she was working at Topstyle?' I was going for a bonus of another lead.

'She was staying with Ferdie; you say you've met him, hey? Well, most of the time she boarded with a family in Manenberg.'

'Do you know where? Could I go and see them?'

'. . . Yes, I know the family quite well. I'll ask them for you.'

'Couldn't I meet them myself?'

'No, I'll ask them. They're a bit funny, you know. If they've got anything to say, I'll tell you and then you can meet. Turn right at the next road.'

'Okay.' And with that I had to be satisfied, as I left my phone number for the third time that day.

CHAPTER 5

As I drove back to my flat, I knew I should have been sorting through the events of the past day in order not to forget anything and to give Van Wyk a coherent account. But I must admit my thoughts were frankly (sickly?) feminine. I was looking forward to the evening ahead; Van Wyk's first appearance at my flat. I was feeling libidinous, probably from the dagga – the effects of which were definitely drifting off. A bath and hair wash were absolutely on, plus a touch of the better of the two perfumes I owned. I had a kind of gypsy-style skirt which suited me quite well. But what to wear with it? A bra was out, I thought (maybe pants too?).

I was just rinsing my hair when the bell went. Oh shit, I whined to myself, was that Van Wyk already – half an hour early, and me in my gown still!!

I peeped through a few inches of opened door.

'Good evening, Miss Cummings?' The visitor was a tall, slim blond man in a suit, with gold-rimmed glasses and short hair. He looked like an advertising executive.

'May we come in for a moment?' I opened the door a bit further and saw another one in an open-neck shirt and lumber-jacket – definitely a thuggish type.

'I don't think so,' I said. 'I'm not dressed. What do you want?'

'My name is Kaplan. I'm from the Bureau of State Security.'

I gaped. A real live agent from BOSS. 'Prove it,' I said cunningly.

'Ah, we don't carry identification,' he said with a grin. 'But perhaps this will do: Kerneels, show her your card.' The thug produced an ID disc which identified him as Kerneels Cronje, sergeant of the Security Police.

'Come in,' I said, feeling a strange mixture of weariness and sheer terror. What did they want? What had I done? What did they think I'd done?

Kaplan settled himself on the soft chair, peered at me, smiling a little. I perched on the corner of my bed, while Cronje leant against the wall, gazing around the room inquisitively.

'You're a medical student, aren't you? In a way I envy you. You know I nearly did medicine myself. It was my late grandfather's dying wish. But in the end I felt the pull to political science too strongly.'

What was this irrelevant nonsense? Had I asked for his curriculum vitae?

'Oh really? How interesting. I nearly did politics. Maybe the two disciplines are related, medicine is a social science, isn't it? You studied at Stellenbosch?'

'Yes. And for a while under Althoesser at the Sorbonne.' There was a short pause. Cronje had begun peering up and down, looking at my books, lifting up papers and magazines on my desk. In a minute he would open drawers, I was certain. Kaplan smiled at me.

'What do you want?' I asked them abruptly.

'Ah, I'll be brief. We have reason to believe that you are searching for a certain Rienet Arendse. Not only searching, but we believe you have made some progress in your attempts to locate her. You may even have made contact with her already. Have you?'

I shook my head. He had asked in a self-deprecatory fashion as if to say: see we don't know everything. But he knew I hadn't met Rienet. And I knew he knew. And he knew, and so on.

'So what we want you to do if you meet her, or hear where she is, is to tell us.'

'Why?'

'We have reason to believe that she may have information about people who are a threat to the security of the state.'

'Who are these people?'

'I am not at liberty to divulge that information.'

'What kind of threat are they?'

'I am not at liberty to divulge that either.'

'Where did you hear that I was looking for her?' Cronje tossed the papers he'd been reading on to the desk with an explosive 'shh' through his lips and gave Kaplan an appealing look, as if to say: let's beat her head in.

'Come, come Miss Cummings, would you trust me if I divulged my sources of information at the drop of a hat?'

'Why don't you investigate her yourselves?'

'Sometimes, Miss Cummings, the industrious and unaligned amateur gets results far quicker than the experienced professional. Also, this is almost a side branch of a big case I'm working on at the moment. So it's not of the highest priority. But that doesn't mean we're not interested in the pursuit of this line. Nor that it can't be moved up the list of priorities.'

'Surely you can't expect me to work for you, if you don't even give me an inkling as to what's going on, Sergeant Kaplan?'

'Oh, you're not working for us. You're helping us. There's a difference, you know. And it's Mr Kaplan. Sergeant Cronje, but Mr Kaplan. Look at it this way: you see before you two accredited representatives of the primary organs responsible for maintaining the security of the state. And we say to you, in the name of the state, that your co-operation is essential. How dare you refuse?' He was smiling again at the implied threat. Oh Christ! Van Wyk would be here any minute. What would the two of them do to a black man? Kaplan might let Cronje stomp

47

all over him just for practice. Promise them anything but just get them out of here, Carol.

'Well, as you're probably aware, all my efforts to find Rienet have lead nowhere so far. But I intend to keep trying and if I find anything useful I'll let you know. Now I really am going out, so if you'll just excuse me . . . Right, nice to have met you Mr Kaplan, do come around again, and bring your friend Mr . . .' I ushered them to the door, flapping my arms like a hen.

At the threshold Cronje spoke for the first time. 'Your eyes are very red.'

'Yours are not so hot either, Cowboy', I snapped back.

'You can call me at this number,' said Kaplan, mechanically handing me a card. 'We want to know: one, where Rienet is; two, if and where you are going to see her; three, the names of all her current friends and where they can be found; and four, anything else you think might interest us. We'll meet again, Miss Cummings.'

'Looking forward to it,' I vamped at their departing backs.

I leant against the door feeling haggard. I rushed into the bedroom to change. The door bell rang. Not them again, could it be? I flung open the door, and there was Van Wyk wearing a bottle of wine and a lascivious grin. I dragged him inside, slammed the door, and buried my nose in his neck. 'Oh Chocolate, where were you when you were positively the last person in the world I wanted to see?'

'Hey?' he said.

'Feeling better, now?'

'Mmm.' We were lying in bed, and Van Wyk was rubbing my back.

'Good. Then let's talk about the day.' He rolled over on his back and put his hands behind his head. 'First of all, these secret policemen. As far as I know, it's rare for BOSS and security men to do the same work. BOSS men tend to be planners, thinkers, co-ordinators. They advise government departments and private institutions. They plan, it's thought, most of government foreign policy. They're responsible directly to the Prime Minister's office and so help to weight his hand in internal wrangles with the big three ministries: Police, Defence and Interior. So in this case, we must wonder why the BOSS man is doing legwork with the secret police. It's the secret police who do the donkey work: investigation, interrogation, infiltration, setting up the spy networks, murder, assassination, and so on. Yet here they appear on your doorstep, apparently working together on a small lead.'

'Well he, Kaplan, did say that it was part of a big case he was working on. And he was definitely in command. Cronje only spoke one sentence to me.'

'Precisely.' Van Wyk waggled his finger in the air for emphasis. 'This is what I'm leading up to: if this had been a case, say, of industrial sabotage as you suspect, Cronje and a buddy would have fetched you down to the police cells, kept you a day or two, interrogated you in detail, slapped you round a bit perhaps, and released you when they felt you had nothing more to tell them. Yet instead, around comes the smooth young Kaplan – not just an ordinary BOSS man but someone who has studied under Althoesser – the whizz kid of the department probably, an expert on Marxist theory. Why? What can he want? Obviously this Rienet business, far from being a sideline of his big case, must be very important. So he does the nice guy act and tries to get you to work for him.'

'Not work, help him,' I muttered.

'And he must need you because the other techniques the secret police have at their disposal – infiltration and intimidation – can't get through to Rienet or whomever. So no matter what you do next, you can expect to see him again very shortly. We must be careful from now on. You could be watched, you know.' He ran one finger down my back and insinuated it between my buttocks.

'Nah, I've heard that the police are de-emphasizing the Immorality Act now.'

'Well, I'm in no hurry to put it to the test. I'll be frank with you. I'd prefer it if they didn't know I knew you.'

'Chocolate, are you preparing to dump me?' I turned over angrily.

'No, no, I'm just saying we've got to be careful. Anyway, I'm waiting for you to say I'm the greatest you've had.' He kissed my shoulder soothingly. I let myself be calmed down. I was feeling rather vulnerable suddenly.

'Well, you were near the greatest tonight. Kind of Joe Frazier standard.'

'Practice, practice, practice, as Angelo Dundee said. Let's not get side-tracked. The Topstyle lead was interesting. So Rienet invented the slogan, "The majority is shit". What could be more anti-democratic than that?'

'But it was over the issue of creches which affected only a minority of workers,' I protested.

'Then they should have convinced the majority of the importance of creches – or accepted the decision of the meeting. How can you have a vocal minority who, every time they don't get their way, abuse the other workers? It's a recipe for anarchy. And then when Rienet gets fired she burns down the factory – one further step along the road of adventurism. I wonder how the other workers felt about losing two weeks' pay.'

'Well, we don't know for sure she was responsible for the fire.'

'We can guess. That woman is an opportunist through and through. And she's dangerous, even to someone who looks for her innocently. You know Carol, I'm with you in whatever you decide to do. But in this case, the more you succeed the more you're bound to fail. The closer you get to Rienet, the more these pigs are going to lean on you. And what of Rienet? If the secret police want to speak to her badly, whatever she's done, you can be damn sure she doesn't want to meet them. So if you pursue

her, you could endanger her – or anyone else who's close
to her.'

'You mean I should forget her,' I said dully. I felt as though
there was a heavy weight on my chest. My oscillating mood of
the past hours had finally slotted into place – one of severe
depression.

'This is the big league, sweetheart,' Van Wyk stroked my hair
lightly. 'And both sides don't stuff around. If you get in their
way, they'll swat you like a fly.'

I lay in silence for a while. Sighed. 'That was deliberate,
wasn't it?'

'What?'

'That imitation of Bogart.'

'Who's Bogart?' he asked, not laughing at all.

The next weekend was one of furious activity. Under Van Wyk's
urging we behaved like a 'normal' couple. That is, we made love,
got drunk, went to a party on Saturday night, a play in the
Townships on Sunday, drove out into the country and picnicked,
fought, made love again, and generally pursued happiness with
the single-mindedness of people with something at the back of
their minds. I suppose in a few years the memory of it will dull in
my mind. But as I look back at it now, I remember each detail of
the weekend with piercing clarity.

The party was given by one of Van Wyk's teachers and fellow
travellers, and though the Great Man's name was never spoken,
I assumed that all those present were Trotskyites.

'Nice place this comrade's got,' I said to Van Wyk as we sat on
the patio in front of the swimming pool. It was a windy but clear
evening, and Table Mountain brooded on the far side of the rose
garden.

'Don't be snide,' he said. 'Class position is not the same as
economic status. Ideology is also important.'

'I just said he had a nice place. I envy him.' I meant it too.

51

Much of the conversation revolved around Poulantzas. I had heard of the name.

'Have you read Gramsci's *Prison Notebooks*?' someone asked me.

'Oh, he's been to prison? I thought he was centre-forward for Real Madrid!'

But the second jug of wine was finished, nobody was even listening to my replies. I was befriended by a great plump pear of a man called Andrew who told me that he preferred dancing to talking shit about politics. While we were dancing he told me that he preferred doodling to dancing. I said dancing was fine for me. He then went off on a long exposition, from the foreign policy of the South African Government since the war, to the struggle between National and International Capital. It was all very comprehensive and built-up like a pyramid, balancing one definition or concept on another. And when it had finished and he/we had got to the pinnacle, still oscillating our behinds to the music, he gripping my buttocks with one huge limp hand absent-mindedly, I asked, 'Andrew, what does the phrase "the sea in which the fishes swim" mean?'

'It's a Maoist epigram – it compares the peasantry to the sea and the rural guerrillas to the fish. I think it might have been coined by Mao himself. Why?'

'Oh, nothing. I just read it somewhere.' We rolled on.

No word was spoken between Van Wyk and me about the Rienet business. I spent the night at his house for a change – I had established a rapport of some kind with his portly landlady, a jewel astonishingly free of social hang-ups, and enjoyed a memorable night in his arms.

'You know,' I said as he drove me home late on Sunday night. 'It's strange. We've spent the whole weekend together, and not once have we had any trouble about race. Do you think we could always have done this, or are things easing up, in Cape Town at least?'

52

'Well, we are of the same class after all. And I think it is true that it's less dangerous now than before. The struggle is an economic one, remember. The ruling fraction of capital is being nudged in the direction of easing racial barriers – what the petit bourgeoisie used to call petty apartheid. I think the mining fraction of capital, the Progressives, are right when they say the ruling fraction is increasingly adopting Progressive policies, that is, rule by the bourgeoisie of whatever race. And they will continue to do so, bearing in mind that Afrikaner capital will always receive preferential treatment.'

'Just let me get this straight: ruling fraction equals Nationalist Party, is that right?'

'Yes.'

'Why don't you Trots call a spade a spade?'

'We prefer to call a spade a disenfranchised but unfree proletarian.'

'Anyway, I'd rather dance than talk shit about politics; and I'd rather doodle than dance.' I snuggled up to his shoulder.

'What about Rienet?' he asked abruptly.

'I dunno. I'll think about her – and them – tomorrow.'

And that's what I did. I went to bed as soon as I got home and slept soundly till morning; my head filled now more with the problem of whether I was falling in love with Van Wyk than with how to find that accursed woman.

CHAPTER 6

The next morning I rose early, feeling wonderful. I showered, washed my hair, chose my clothes with some care and spent the whole day at medical school. Allan took me aside as I was leaving that evening.

'Carrie, you're looking great, you really are.'

'Why, thank you, Allan, it's sweet of you to remark on it.'

'No, Carrie, you're looking as though all your troubles are behind. In fact, "well-fucked" is the phrase I had in mind. I hope you don't mind me saying so.'

I swelled with warmth for this brash idiot. 'No I don't mind. You should try it yourself sometime.'

Allan had been living sadomasochistically for several years with Jenny, a clumsy girl with massive breasts. 'Ay,' he said, shaking his head.

Martin was waiting for me outside my car. For once, I barely noticed his student's coat, very starched and very white, with its chic assorted tools of the doctor's trade – a hammer, various lights and scopes, a stethoscope – protruding from his pockets.

'Hi, Carol,' he began.

'Yes?' I said briskly. It was now after five, and I reckoned I had spent more than enough time at the hospital for one day.

'How's the work going?' It was clear that Martin wanted something. I hoped to cut short his run-up by climbing into my car and muttering, 'Fine, fine.'

'Um, Carol, my cousin Benjie is taking me out for dinner next Tuesday and I wondered if you'd like to come along.'

I was shaken by this. What a bouncer! After all these years, Martin was asking for a date.

'Fine. Great. Thanks for asking. See you Tuesday.'

Well, well. Everybody loves a winner, I thought as I drove off. But what about Van Wyk? Was I not falling in love with him? It's only a date, I told myself, and anyway I deserve it after panting after Martin for two years.

I returned to my flat bursting with energy. I intended to clean it thoroughly and then get very engrossed in liver disease (Van Wyk had a meeting). The phone rang. Just as I picked it up, I got that feeling again, that sense of foreboding, like an aeroplane flying across my soul.

'Hello Carol, this is Amien Sonday. I've been trying to get you the whole weekend. I heard about Rienet. Apparently she was hanged earlier this year for killing a shopowner – bad trend that hey, ha ha? No really, it's true. Came as quite a shock when I first heard it. But she always was a wild one. I suppose it was with that Ferdie Marten's gang. They were big gangsters.'

'How did it happen?' I asked.

'Apparently,' – where was it I'd read that people who say apparently or frankly or honestly a lot are always lying? – 'apparently they held up this store, a jewellery store I think it was, and then shot the owner as they were leaving. All four of them got the rope. Funny, I don't remember seeing it in the papers – probably happened while I was in Mecca.'

I thanked him and put the phone down quietly. Of course I knew it wasn't true. I knew it emotionally, intellectually, intuitively. But I also knew because there'd been no record of her name in births and deaths. The question was, was Sonday an unwitting tool in passing on false information? Or was he a deceiving tool deliberately providing false information?

I didn't have to ponder very long because just then Ferdie Martens rang.

'I've been trying to reach you all weekend,' he said reprovingly. On the telephone all his sinister ambience seemed increased somehow. 'I heard about Rienet. She's trying for white up in Port Elizabeth, living with some Trust Bank executive.'

'Oh,' I said. 'Are you sure?'

'My information is usually reliable. They say she doesn't want to be reminded of her Capey background. Talks lah-de-da, drives a sports car.'

'Um,' I said. 'Thank you then.'

And, of course, half an hour later Mrs Isaacs rang to say that Rienet had moved to Britain, where she was a very successful model.

So my three leads had all come back with stories designed to make me stop looking for Rienet; three different stories, so they couldn't have originated from the same place. The three different informants couldn't have begged for time to 'ask around' as they had claimed, because if they had checked with Rienet (or someone close to her), they would have got their act together. So the only explanation was that all three must have needed time to concoct a seemingly unverifiable story. Unless, of course, all three stories were circulating about Rienet at the same time. Maybe she had already become a legendary figure, a Boadicea about whom fact and fiction could no longer be separated? No, that was tripe!

Therefore: my three leads must all have knowingly attempted to mislead me. And, therefore, it was safe to assume they also knew a bit more about Rienet.

Which one to approach now? Not Furtive Ferdie, nor sweet Mrs Isaacs, if it could be helped. I was starting to get that Rienet-hunting frenzy.

'Hello Amien? Carol. Look, I want you to stop this fucking

bullshit about Rienet. I want to see her and I want to see her this evening, or I'm going around in the morning to start orthodox enquiries, know what I mean?' I screamed menacingly into the inert receiver.

There was a long pause.

'I'll ring you back in a few minutes,' he said.

I glowed with expectation and triumph. Maybe I might crack the case tonight even?

He rang back in exactly 12 minutes. 'Drive in to Elsies River. Park your car at the railway bridge and walk towards my shop. Some friends will pick you up and take you to Rienet. I won't be there. Goodbye.'

I rushed out of the house and drove like a madwoman to Elsies River. My pulse was pounding and I was almost gasping as I strode along towards Sonday's Bazaar. A car drew up next to me. 'Are you Rienet's friend?' asked the driver, a thin youth with tattoos over poorly developed forearms. I got in the back next to a very young lad with pimples – he looked no more than 16. He kept staring at my body, then looking away in embarrassment whenever I caught him at it. The third guy in the passenger seat was thick-set and fleshy and ignored me. They all had moustaches.

'Is it far?' I asked.

'Not far,' said the driver shortly.

We drove along in silence, heading out towards Bellville. We turned off the main drag on to a single lane tarmac and then a minute or two later onto a dirt road. My anticipation was giving way rapidly to fear. I chided myself mentally for a typical white female South African reaction; I tried to think what Rienet herself would be feeling in this situation. I felt a bit more relaxed as we stopped. When the lights were switched off, we were surrounded by a blackness illuminated on one side by the nearby orange glow of a highway.

'Is Rienet here?' I asked.

57

'Ja', said the driver. The three of them opened the doors and got out. I scrambled out after them. The young one held the door for me as I got out, his hot eyes on my breasts. They stood around me in a semi-circle, the other two deferring to the scrawny tattooed driver.

'Well?' I said briskly.

The tattooed one hit me across the side of my head with his fist. I crashed against the car, and bounced upright again. 'Hey!' I shouted, my voice high pitched and feminine.

'Well, you bitch,' he said, hitting me again. He pronounced it 'bits'.

'Well? Well?' he kept asking as he swung his fists at me. I turned to run, but one of the others tripped me, and I fell sprawling on the cool sand.

'Rienet this and Rienet that, hey? Bits!' He lashed out at me with his feet. 'Going to call the fucking cops, were you? You white bits!' And then, with horror, I saw him begin to undo his trousers. Oh God, no, I screamed to myself. This can't be happening. It can't be. I tried to scramble away, but other hands held me down. Someone fumbled with the buckle of my jeans and then ripped them off me with my panties as well. No. No. I kept on screaming, begging them, cursing them, vowing vengeance. I remembered somewhere that rape requires a degree of volition on the part of the victim. I pulled my legs up to my chest. The tattooed one muttered an oath, knelt in front of me and began to pummel my face and head in earnest. I remembered then that some police brigadier had also advised victims not to resist too much. My head was really ringing now and I could taste blood in my mouth. With the other two holding my arms, I lowered my legs in a final capitulation. And then, Jesus Christ! I thought at first he'd stuck his knee up my vagina. He thrashed around briefly and then ejaculated with an oath. He got off me and I half raised myself on my arms when the thick-set, silent one came around to the business end of me. 'My

58

chance,' he said with a grin. He lifted up my jersey and ripped of my bra. 'God, look at those tits!' he said, pawing them brutally. A real romantic, he began to stick his disgustingly foul-smelling tongue in my mouth. Eventually he got on the job as well, entered me with a brief moment of agony, then came his load and floundered around like a beached fish.

It was the lad's chance now. The thick-set one took up his position at my shoulder. The boy lowered himself on to me gingerly. I was awash with the semen of those other two pigs so I hardly felt him enter me. He gyrated around for some time, maybe two minutes, I wasn't feeling a thing now. I think he must have had erection troubles, what with his two colleagues looking on. Or maybe it was his first time, I don't know. Anyway, he studiously ignored my body, just pumping away manfully.

'Oh Christ, hurry up won't you?' I moaned. I felt him shrivelling up inside me. He gave a convulsive moan, faked an orgasm and then pulled himself off.

The three of them got back in the car. 'Next time we'll slice your tits off, you fucking bits,' spat the tattoo, and they roared off in a cloud of wheelspin.

I lay there in the darkness weeping softly, till the chill night air began to seep into my limbs. Then I got up feeling stiff and sore, my head throbbing, and dressed slowly.

As I trudged slowly back along the road, crying and aching, I consoled myself with thinking of various punishments for the three louts, but most of all for Amien Sonday.

I was going to make that rat pay – and how.

CHAPTER 7

I must have walked along that road for two or three hours before I managed to hike a lift back with a middle-aged couple. I told them I'd been raped, shamelessly exploiting my predicament to get them to drop me back at my car – quite a bit out of their way. They wanted to drop me at the police station, but I assured them I wanted to speak to my mother first. In fact, as I started the car up, I suddenly realized how much I would like to speak to my mother, and for a moment I had a wild desire to put through an R20 call to her, a thousand miles away in Johannesburg. Then I remembered how difficult it was for her to understand such mundane things as wanting to study in Cape Town or wearing boots, let alone anything more complex.

I got back to the flat close to three in the morning and locked myself securely in. I made myself a cup of coffee and then let myself cry. I wept in anger and self-pity, in frustration and hurt; and suddenly in quite soul-stretching loneliness. After quite a bit of that, I pulled myself together with an effort, had a long shower and surveyed the damage to my body. In fact, once the dirt was washed off, it was surprisingly slight. My face was quite bruised and swollen, and I had a puffy cut lip. There were more bruises on my arms and shoulders and a couple of really nasty ones on my ribs which felt as if there were fractures underneath. There was a long scratch over one breast and there was a very slight vaginal tear that looked as though it would heal by itself. My groin area ached quite a bit. But other than that, physically I felt quite well. As for mentally . . . I felt as though I'd climbed a mountain or run a road race – mainly pleased it was all over. Paradoxically, I was almost a little proud, as though I'd finally attained womanhood – after all I'd been gang-raped and beaten up only a few hours before. I had experienced the worst that could happen to any woman – and survived. Then I remembered small details from the assault – the sight of tattoo's penis, the feel of his fists thudding into my head, the way the thick-set one's tongue has snaked in and out of his greasy mouth – and I began to feel nauseous and faint. God, what if they'd made me suck them off? This was too much for my supra-tentorial stomach and I rushed to the bathroom to vomit up the coffee.

When I got back, I unearthed a packet of cigarettes and smoked several, enjoying the light-headedness after long withdrawal. I lay in a bubble bath for a long time, soaping and re-soaping my body as though it were something alien to me.

Then I tried to sleep, but couldn't. I wanted badly to talk to someone. I nearly dialled Van Wyk several times but I knew it shouldn't be a man. Unfortunately I've always had difficulty making female friends. All my friends, even now, are men. Well, there was Suzy whom I had known for years, but she was married now, and expecting, and I hadn't seen her for ages. And then there was Christine in my class at medical school, but she could only just be called a friend. For me to burden her with my tales of woe would be inappropriate.

The sky was just getting light when I thought of Chocolate's landlady. It was still another couple of hours before she'd have the house to herself so I had another shower, drove into town and bought a takeaway at a dingy working-class café. Then I drove up Signal Hill and in the stark, early morning light, the bay still covered in mist, watched the sun rise, sticky-fingering sausages and chips in contentment. It was so romantic I was surprised to find myself crying again. This time I experienced mostly a sense of loss rather than anger or pain.

Van Wyk's landlady was only slightly surprised to see me. When I told her of my latest experience (discreetly, I thought, avoiding any mention of Rienet – although, with hindsight, this was a mistake) she accepted her role of mother-surrogate with great verve. We clasped each other emotionally, and she told me of a similar experience in her youth. She understood completely my reluctance to see Van Wyk for the moment; also, though for the wrong reasons obviously, my reticence in going to the police. 'Those robbises! They don't help you. They just make a fool of you all over again. No, you waste your time with them. But if you ever see those vuilgats that did this to you, you come and tell me. My husband's got a couple of friends who would know how to handle scum like that.' She urged me to go away to family for a few days. 'Ernest will wait,' she said simply.

And so, with her twin concepts of revenge and retreat in my mind, I planned my next moves.

I left a note for Van Wyk, saying I had to go away for a few days. Then I went to the bank and drew out R250, thinking a little ashamedly, 'Daddy will pay' – as he would, out of the surplus extracted from his underpaid construction workers. Then I went along to a gun shop and with surprising ease – they even had the licence form there – bought a .32-calibre pistol. How simple for a young white princess! Just pay your money and select your weapon; go out and blow somebody's head off, do you think anybody cares? The gun was a good size. It fitted neatly into my hand, smooth and cold like a snake. It didn't remind me a bit of a phallus but then I can only speak consciously. The assistant enthused greatly about its suitability as a woman's gun; and when I pointed out that it was much smaller than Clint Eastwood's he assured me it would stop a charging elephant. I had no interest in elephants, but I took the gun with a chic little holster that could be worn around my waist or shoulder. I got a few boxes of ammunition with the change and, delighted by my new toy, spent the rest of the morning at an indoor shooting range. I never attained any particular accuracy with my dildo but I at least learnt to handle it confidently and not jump when I pulled the trigger.

Then I leapt into my car (yes leapt; I was definitely feeling more and more like a Hollywood policeman) and drove slowly up the coast to Gansbaai, a little coastal village about 150 miles from Cape Town. I arrived there that evening and got the few interested stares that single girls always get when I checked into the hotel. For once, though, with my pistol nudging into my armpit as I walked, the attention did not ruffle my confidence.

I spent the next two days at Gansbaai, lazing on the beach in the spring sunshine, having a couple of drinks after dinner before going to bed early. With my window open, I could hear the sound of the sea half a mile away just before I slipped into a deep, dreamless sleep. I had taken John Fowles's *The Magus* with me, and read it slowly and deliberately on the beach. I read with total absorption; enjoyed being carried away from my obsessions by another character's.

Slowly, over the days of my 'convalescence,' my body straightened itself out. The cuts and bruises faded – except for one over my ribs where a sharp intake of breath could still remind me of the fracture underneath. The swelling of my face receded, and in the warm, but not hot, sun my skin turned a golden colour. My hair, too, was assailed by sun and salt and became a couple of shades lighter. The sea had gradually purged me of my bathing compulsion although I did have five my first day there. I spoke to no one besides the waiters at the hotel and one beach-blond young surfer. He had been eyeing me the whole morning of the second day and by lunchtime had screwed up enough nerve to approach me. He shambled across the sand, loose-limbed and straggly, while I mentally willed him to go away.

'Hey,' he said with an engaging smile, 'weren't you in Plet a couple of weeks ago?' I rolled over on to my back and pulled out my pistol from underneath my clothes.

'Get lost, creep, or I'll blow your head off,' I snarled. The effect was electrifying. He muttered an apology and retreated wide-eyed, so scared and humiliated that he couldn't walk properly. A petty victory, I thought, replacing my gun, but a victory nevertheless, in a week when there hadn't been many.

I finished *The Magus* on the afternoon of the second day – didn't really understand the moral, something to do with personal freedom or some such. Not terribly relevant to my situation, I thought, but a rattling good story.

And so the next day, refreshed in mind and body, I returned to Cape Town, feeling much like Marlon Brando after practising shooting with his left hand in a mine shaft in *One-Eyed Jacks*.

I stopped for a cup of coffee in the city centre and bought a newspaper. Same old stories: civilians killed in cross fire in Rhodesia; Miss World contest to be renamed Ms World; a bank hold-up in Sea Point where the robbers had scattered ANC pamphlets after them – that was new.

I hadn't given my quest much thought in Gansbaai. I felt strong and confident and was going to be direct from now on. I too, had suffered some in my search for Rienet and I wasn't going to be fobbed off with variations of the you-have-no-right-to-meet-Rienet theme. As for my revenge on Amien Sonday – I hadn't forgotten that insect, but there was no hurry for that. I'd wait a while, let him put his guard down and then zap him.

'Hey there, white goose!' said Jasper in recognition.

'I want to see Ferdie, please,' I said, working on my menacing tone in practice for the big confrontation. I waited in the little office for maybe five minutes, my tension rising steadily. Then Ferdie came in, stumping awkwardly across the linoed floor. He nodded a greeting at me as he sunk into a chair.

'What now?' he asked, making eye contact immediately.

I pulled out my dildo from my waistband and levelled it at his nose. 'Find me Rienet or I'll blow your head off.' Ferdie leaned back in his chair. And chuckled.

'What's eating you, whitey? I told you Rienet was in Port Elizabeth, didn't I?'

'Yes, you did. And Amien Sonday told me she was dead, hanged. And someone else told me she was in London.'

'So? They were wrong.'

'When I challenged Sonday about it, he lured me to a deserted spot in Bellville and had me beaten and raped by three of his henchmen. I'm not playing games anymore, Ferdie. I can't trust any of you.'

He leant forward in his chair, ran his hands through his short curly hair for a while. 'I'm sorry, Carol. You know I had nothing to do with that. Put that gun away and let's be calm about this.' I hesitantly replaced the gun in its holster. Until that moment, when he denied it, the thought had never crossed my mind that Ferdie might be in this with Amien Sonday. Maybe they had arranged it together. Ferdie would be able to get hold of three bully boys much more easily than the legitimate shopowner. Why the different stories then? To lure me on? To confuse me?

'What would you have done if I'd phoned you instead of Sonday?' I asked.

'I don't go in for rape much these days. If I'd had to make my own decision, I suppose I would have had you killed.' He spoke flatly, stating a simple fact. I gaped at him. I'd come in flashing a revolver around, and now a minute later he was quite composed, and I was quaking in terror.

'Look, we must sort this thing out once and for all. I'll try to get a final answer within a couple of days. In the meantime don't do any more running around and waving guns and threatening. Just be patient. Wait for me to contact you. Don't tell anyone about this. Who else knows you've seen me – a lot of people?'

'No, just one. My lover.'

'He will keep it to himself?'

'I'm sure he will.'

'Good, so just go home to your nice flat in Newlands and relax. I'll be in touch in a few days . . .'

'How do you know I live in Newlands?'

'You told me.'

'I didn't.'

'Okay. We found out,' he snapped.

Another shock. So now I had been investigated by Ferdie's 'we' as well as by the Secret Police. Or were they one and the same? The police often used criminal elements to do their dirty work. Could Ferdie be working for them? He was ruthless enough. But then why all this footsie-footsie about Rienet? I tried another tack.

'Did Amien Sonday make his decision on his own as well?'

'I suppose so.'

'Then you're both in the same organization?'

'There is no organization. There is no connection between Sonday and myself or between him and . . . anybody else.'

'And between you and anybody else? Why do I have to wait for two days to hear from Rienet?'

'You ask too many fucking questions. These things take time. I have to consult with my superiors.' He closed his lips firmly as if he'd said too much. We were silent for a few moments, both of us considering his pompous-sounding statement. I got up to go.

'How do I know you won't decide to kill me after all?'

'I don't think that will be necessary. But if, if I should suddenly get a visit from the vuiles,' (he used the Afrikaans word for police, literally filth, filthy ones), 'you won't live out the week. Keep absolutely quiet about all this. And don't visit me here again. I'll contact you.

'Oh Carol, one more thing. Never point a gun, if you don't mean to use it.'

'I was going to use it.'

'No you weren't.' Ferdie was almost smiling.

I left.

Only later did I remember that I should have told Ferdie about Kaplan and Cronje; that they must have been snooping around someone that I had been to see. What if they tired of waiting for leads from me and decided to pull him in for questioning? Would he turn his boys loose on me?

Just a few short weeks ago, I had been a self-indulgent, shrill female medical student who considered herself a radical thinker. Now, what had begun as an innocent quest and developed into an obsession (so what? I had had other obsessions before) was confronting me with do-or-die alternatives. I had been beaten up and raped; threatened with murder (was still being threatened with murder); threatened by the Secret Police; had fallen in love (illicitly); for what? I wanted to meet Rienet badly – but not this badly. I played with the laughing Jesus idly. It had become so much a part of my body that I hardly noticed it anymore. I sighed. Everything was out of my hands now; I had to wait for other people to move.

I decided to spend the few hours that needed killing, before Van Wyk got home, at my flat. I tried to tidy it again, forcing myself to look at things as an outsider would. Once a pile of clothes has been in a certain spot for a week it becomes like furniture – so long as it does not fall over, it is right and in no need of moving. I hummed a little as I shoved shoes under the bed. Where do other people keep their shoes?

The doorbell rang and my heart fluttered a little – Van Wyk? Kaplan? Ferdie? Rienet? My pulse began to pound. I took a deep breath.

'Darling! I tried you earlier but you were out. Here, put these in a vase before they wilt.'

'Oh, Mum,' I said weakly.

I wandered across the flat with the bunch of carnations in my hand as my mother bustled in with a small suitcase. A suitcase?

Oh my God, she is not planning . . .

'I'm in Cape Town for two days for an orchid conference so I thought I'd stay with you rather than a hotel. Is that all right, darling? How are things at medical school? When do exams start? Have you made any progress with that nice Jewish boy, what's his name? Russell, is it? Do you know what your father said to me the other day? . . .'

I dumped the flowers in an empty milk bottle, which was the closest thing to a vase I was likely to find, and shrank back on to my bed. I could not believe that a few days previously I had actually considered confiding that I'd been raped to this loud, overactive stranger. More than anything else, I did not want to spend two evenings with my mother. She would want to trade schoolgirl confessions into the night. I imagined myself making up another whole life to satisfy her – going to parties, boys I had been out with, interesting cases, medical ones, that is, that I had solved. It all seemed so unfair. Surely I did not deserve this after all I had been through in the past week.

'. . . "I'm sick and tired of all your moaning," I said to him. "You've become a cliché the way you complain about the servants." ' Mother had, in a very short time, assembled a tea tray with a pot, cups and some biscuits she had brought with her. The kettle hissed menacingly in the kitchenette. 'So,' she said, 'tell me all. When are exams? Are you confident?'

'They're three weeks away. I'm a little further behind than usual but apparently everyone passes fifth year, so I suppose I'll be okay.'

'Mmh. Then off to London for three months, you lucky thing you. Ursula's son, Garth, is at the Royal Free. I'll get you his address before you go. Perhaps she can phone him and ask him to book you into some shows. Even in winter it's difficult to get tickets sometimes.'

'Mum, please. I'll make my own arrangements for London. I'm going to be working some of the time, anyhow.'

'Well, we can argue that one later. Your flat could do with a bit of a clean up. Perhaps I'll get stuck in tomorrow morning before I go to the conference.'

'You know the flat's very small for two people. Are you sure you'll be comfortable here?'

'But, Carol, we can sleep together in this big bed. We've done it before!' My mother was assuming a hurt expression. I thought guiltily of the stains on the bed. I'd have to change the sheets surreptitiously.

'Do you not want me to stay? Do you have a new boyfriend?'

'Well, yes, I am having a relationship at the moment. Well, actually, it is not really a relationship, it's . . .' I trailed off. I'd made a mistake in thinking that my mother would leave discreetly if I mentioned I had a lover. My father became angry at the thought of boyfriends; mother got vicariously interested.

'Who is he, darling? Are you in love?'

'Look I don't want to talk about it.'

'Don't be so secretive. Come on, tell me.'

'I don't wish to discuss this.'

'Come on, Carol. Don't be silly. I won't tell your father.'

'Mother!' I shrieked at her. 'Will you leave me alone! I am not prepared to discuss this. Three days ago I was . . .' The doorbell rang and saved me from further indiscretion.

It was Van Wyk. 'I was only 10 miles to a point where I'd be passing your flat so I thought I'd drop in. Where've you been?'

I wiggled my eyebrows in desperate warning to him. He cocked his head to one side in reply.

'Mr Van Wyk, how are you? Come inside and meet my mother.'

Van Wyk oozed charm all over Mum. 'The resemblance is unmistakable,' he said, shaking her hand firmly.

She insisted he stayed to tea. He held his cup with his pinky extended, trying to be funny when I wasn't in the mood. He explained to my mother that we had met at a student clinic, 'offering a much-needed service to my community'.

'That's odd,' said Mother. 'In December she told us that student clinics were like charity; that they failed to get to grips with the root causes of disease. Didn't you say that, Carol?'

'I need the practice now,' I said grimly.

'One's got to keep reassessing one's position,' said Van Wyk.

'Look, Mr Van Wyk, I haven't finished those figures that I'd promised you. I'll try to do them tonight and drop them off at your school tomorrow.'

'Oh, right, Carol. Good. No tearing rush with them, in fact. I was just in the area, so I thought I'd see if they were done. I must be off now . . .'

I silently blew Van Wyk a kiss at the door and he responded by feigning a swoon just out of my mother's sight.

Mother was staring into her lap when I came back into the room. When she looked up, I saw her eyes were full of tears.

'You're sleeping with him, aren't you?'

'Mother! What on earth gives you that idea . . .?'

'Don't bother denying it. I can tell. He's the "person" you're involved with. Oh, Carol, you're going to land up in jail. What's your father going to say?'

We argued for over an hour. My mother alternated between wheedling and weeping. She begged me to give him up – not because he was coloured but because it was against the law. I'd end up in jail, humiliated; my name would be dragged through the mud; my career, finished before it had started; my parents, heartbroken.

I vehemently denied that we slept together. We were simply good friends, and there was no law against that.

I became so angry at her jumping to conclusions, and so convinced by my own arguments in defence of platonic relationships across the colour bar, that I began to believe my own lies. How could she accuse me of having sex with Van Wyk

70

when we were simply best of friends? I suppose I was reluctant to credit my mother with any capacity for insight at all, so how could she be right about me and Van Wyk?

When she began to repeat her pleas for what seemed the tenth time, I had had enough.

'Ultimately,' I snapped at her, 'this is none of your damned business. Whatever you say is not going to change my mind. If I can get no support from you, then you might as well go.'

Mother rose regally and took her bag in her hand.

'I shall report this to your father,' she said, and swept out.

'Don't worry. He can cope, I'm sure,' I screamed at her as she slammed the door.

I headed for Van Wyk's house, paused, thought for a while, and decided on a quick shower before leaving, just in case.

'Where did you go?' We were lying side-by-side on the narrow bed, the sweat drying on our bodies.

'To Gansbaai. I just wanted to be alone for a while to think things out. I lay in the sun for two days. It was great.'

'Your tan is very sexy. Did you, uh, go alone?'

'Oh course.' I bit him gently on the smooth curve of his deltoid muscle. I had decided not to tell him of Amien and the rape business. I didn't know how he would react. Would he attempt to avenge me? Confront Amien? Seek out his bully boys? Would he be disgusted? The assault had been on me and me alone; I would decide how and when to retaliate.

'And what about Rienet?'

Ah . . . Rienet. What now? I couldn't very well tell him of the latest developments, while leaving out the rape.

'I've decided not to pursue her anymore. If any of those people I've already met were to come up with something concrete about her – that would be different. But otherwise I'm not going to carry on looking.'

'That's good.' He raised himself on one elbow and peered at

me. 'Really Darling, um, Carol, I think it might be very dangerous for all of us, particularly Rienet, if you go on chasing her.'

I sighed. He was hardly making me feel any more secure about the future. Maybe I should tell him the truth, even now, I thought. He flopped down again. 'That's a load off my mind. Now all you have to do is keep the Secret Police off your back and everything will be fine. You know, I was reading this article yesterday on the working-class movements in Vietnam in the fifties. There are actually quite a lot of parallels with our own problems . . .'

So, I did not tell him that the Rienet quest was not as dead as I had led him to believe.

CHAPTER 8

'Miss Cummings.'

'Mr Kaplan. Come in, I suppose.'

'Thank you. Hot day, isn't it?'

'Very hot . . . yes. Very hot.'

'I suppose you're wondering why I called, hm?'

'Oh, it's not about the weather?'

'No. It's about Rienet Arendse.'

'Oh. I've decided not to look for her any more.'

'Aha. Go on.'

'No, I've finished. That's all I have to say.'

'You seem rather aggressive today, Miss Cummings. Is something wrong? Or is it that Sergeant Cronje isn't with me today and you feel a bit more confident?'

'Possibly. He scares me.'

'It's just his manner. He's a very fine policeman – thorough, methodical, hardworking. Anyway I see you're determined to be uncooperative. Let me tell you a little story – two little stories actually. When I was at the Sorbonne, I went out with someone in my class. A girl, of course . . .'

'Of course.'

'. . . A student from Dahomey. A very beautiful woman – a black woman, you understand. We got on very well. We were very compatible – this was some years before I married.'

'You were both Marxists?'

'You're baiting me, Miss Cummings. Mind if I smoke?' He lit

73

a cigarette. 'Would you say that British Intelligence officers who studied German during the Second World War were Nazis? Anyway, she now has quite an important job in the government back in her own country. I tell you this to illustrate that I'm not one of these people who look down on dark people, who believe they're filth, not worth associating with. I believe that the essential contradiction facing us here in South Africa, as in the rest of the world, is that between free enterprise and communism, with its whole Marxist mythology in various stages of dilution behind it. And I think this view is becoming more and more prevalent among my colleagues. Racial prejudice is becoming a millstone around the neck of the government and the security services. It's on the way out, definitely.'

Pause.

'That's the end of the first story.'

'. . . Interesting.'

'The other goes like this: you've heard of TLSA and NEUM? Teachers' League of South Africa and the Non-European Unity Movement, now just called the Unity Movement of course. The Unity Movement went underground in the 1960s; the TLSA is still a legal organization. They were both Trotskyite front organizations. I suppose you know about Trotskyites – they're completely unable to get on with any other groups; they never make alliances and hate other left-wing parties with the same fervour they hate right-wing parties. Now a fair number of the members of these two organizations have been picked up in the past, but most of them have been left untouched. Oh, we know who they are, mostly coloured school teachers in Cape Town. But we leave them alone for two reasons: first of all because they're inactive; and secondly, because with their rigid approach, they tend to spread confusion among more gullible people that we would prefer to see confused.

'But this I want to emphasize: we know just about all of them, those who have prospered, gone into business and turned their backs on the movements, as well as those who are still having study groups and such like. We, I, can pull them in whenever I like – keep them in for a few weeks or forever if I choose. You see what I'm driving at?'

'Not really.'

'Well, to speak plainly, Miss Cummings, I'm threatening you: find me Rienet Arendse or I'll break your coloured boyfriend's arse. Well, I must be going now. I never get offered any tea here, you know. Cheerio, Miss Cummings, see you soon.'

This latest threat I could obviously not keep from Van Wyk. We discussed it, and the implications, at great length. Clearly I, at least – and possibly Van Wyk, too – was under surveillance (I didn't mention that Ferdie, if he were separate from the Secret Police, had also had some kind of investigation done on me).

Van Wyk wasn't too concerned about being detained. 'I can't claim to be a mature revolutionary if I don't spend some time in jail,' he said, 'and it's unlikely these would be any interrogation – my arrest would just be used as a lever on you. And once I was arrested, the lever would be of no use. No, I think they're more likely to threaten you with it than carry it out. Probably what they'd like to do is catch us in bed together. Then they'd charge us under the Immorality Act and use that as a stick to drive you to Rienet.'

He was becoming far more agitated about my giving up the search for Rienet. 'Now you *know* they're following you, it would be very bad for you to reach Rienet – you'd lead these pigs straight to her. Look, Kaplan's still doing his own legwork. Whatever it is that Rienet's into, it's big. Did you see tonight's paper? There was another bank hold-up – this time there was a shoot-out with the security guards. One of the guards was shot dead and one of the robbers, or guerrillas if you prefer, was wounded but still escaped. They left more ANC pamphlets behind. Could this be it? Is Rienet involved in urban terrorism?'

The question was rhetorical but I answered it anyway. 'Could be,' I said slowly. 'It might be the sort of thing she'd do.'

'Idiot. You've never even met her.'

'Doesn't mean I don't know her.'

'That's true, I suppose.' He gave me a thoughtful look.

'Do you think we should stop seeing each other?' I asked, unashamedly the coquette.

'Nah, what for? To suffer some more? No, we carry on. If they come for me, it's too bad. But we mustn't get caught together in bed. I've a friend who's gone on holiday. We can use his house in Belhar.'

And so we did for the next few nights, weaving circles and dodging in and out of buses in an effort to shake off real or imagined pursuers. We'd arrive at Belhar, a new, bland middle-class coloured township, in different vehicles, enter the house by different routes (me by the front, Van Wyk over the wall and through the back) and after a few minutes' initial paranoia, settle comfortably into a suburban-type togetherness. We would make tea in the small bright kitchen, turn down the candlewick bedspread, and climb into bed with the radio tuned to Springbok.

What surprised me about Van Wyk was that the part of my interview with Kaplan that shook him the most was where he had dismissed the Trots contemptuously. Van Wyk returned to the implications again and again in the night.

'I mean, if the Secret Police themselves say your organization is at best ineffective, at worst actually working to serve their, the police's, interests, then you have to rethink your whole stand. Are we being too uncompromising in dismissing the ANC and SA Communist Party as petit bourgeois? Having branded them as reformists, does it mean we can't work with them? Or at least alongside them? I don't know, I really don't. I think the group must get together and reanalyse our whole stand in detail. In detail,' he repeated, sleepily.

And thus Van Wyk's life, touched on by mine, touched on by Rienet's, was rerouted.

CHAPTER 9

Three days went by. I was in a state of suspended animation (more suspense than animation). The days I spent at medical school, the nights with Van Wyk in Belhar.

I was just picking up my books before school on the fourth morning, when Ferdie rang. 'Meet me outside the Post Office in Claremont in half an hour,' he said brusquely.

I was there on time; he showed up 15 minutes late. 'You're late,' I accused. He ignored it.

'Listen Carol, we need your help. A friend of mine has been badly hurt. An accident. We need some penicillin for him – and any advice you can give. Can you see him tonight? We'll take you to him.'

I was surprised. I had been expecting anything but this.

'Why don't you take him to a doctor?'

'He's in trouble. We can't take him anywhere.'

'Will Reinet be there?'

'Probably not. No. She won't be there.'

'Why should I do this? I want to meet Rienet. I don't want to get mixed up with you and your petty hoodlum friends. Why should I trust you?'

Ferdie's face was impassive, his snakelike eyes resting on mine unblinkingly. I supposed he was angry.

'Don't you have an oath you take? Why . . .'

'No, I don't have an oath – I'm a student, not a doctor.'

'Should we call you in two years' time then?' he sneered. We

78

had begun to raise our voices. We moved back away from the busy pedestrian thoroughfare.

'Why should we trust you?' he went on softly. 'What do we know of you except that you cause to lot of trouble. If you help my friend now, I promise I'll arrange, try to arrange a meeting with Rienet.'

'Is it in your power to arrange a meeting? Can you do it or is this more lies?'

'Rienet meets who she wants to. I can't speak for her. But I'll try to organize it.' What could I say? Could I say no?

'Okay. What kind of accident? Why do you need penicillin?'

'I can't tell you more. It's an accident, and I think it's very infected.'

'What part of his body?'

'His arm.'

'Ferdie, the Secret Police are leaning on me to find Rienet for them.'

'Oh, I know that,' he said casually. 'Just be sure you're not followed tonight. If you meet Rienet, it will be in a place where she won't be found again.'

'Another thing. I've left a letter with my lawyer to be opened if I die suddenly,' I lied glibly, 'pointing a finger at you.'

'Ag, Carol man, you watch too many bleddie films.' He turned to go. 'Anyways,' he threw over his shoulder, 'if I had to kill you I'd have to disappear for a time. We'll meet you here tonight at eight o'clock.'

Curse you, Ferdie, I muttered as he limped off, how do you manage always to get the last word in?

I spent the remainder of the day touring theatre, the wards and the accident unit with my big sling-bag over my shoulder, heading periodically for my car to dump my swag. I didn't know exactly what the problem was but I had a shrewd idea as to what kind of 'accident' I was supposed to treat – presupposing, of course, that it wasn't a hoax. Could Ferdie deliver Rienet? I

79

didn't know. Strangely enough I was growing almost to trust him – he was so frank about his undoubted capacity for violence that it was positively disarming.

At eight that night I began slowly to patrol up and down in front and alongside the Claremont Post Office. The area was deserted and I felt ridiculously exposed with my weighty bag over my shoulder. It was crammed with everything thinkable, short of a portable operating table.

A young girl strolled across and posted a letter. 'Have you got the time, Miss?' she asked politely.

'Um . . . ten past eight.'

'Our car is around the corner, Miss Cummings.' My heart leapt an instant. Rienet? No – too dark, too slim, too tall. I followed her around the side of the building and got into the back of an old Morris Minor. There were two men in the front. The girl got in next to me. I remembered my previous night-time car journey with three strangers.

'Where's Ferdie?' I asked in alarm.

'He's going to meet us there, Carol,' said the driver speaking perfect English. 'Please lie down. We don't want you to see where we're going.'

'Don't be afraid. We're going to blindfold you, but we won't hurt you. Poppie?'

The girl next to me bound up my eyes as I lay cramped on the floor. We seemed to drive for hours, making innumerable twists and turns. At one stage the car made a squealing U-turn and then stopped, facing the way we had come. The engine was switched off and we all sat (or in my case lay) in silence.

'Are we there?' I whispered. 'What's happening?'

'Relax, we're just making sure we weren't followed.' I liked the sound of the driver. Very calm and assured.

We continued on our circuitous course and eventually pulled in somewhere.

'Right, Carol. Poppie's just going to take your gun . . .' I began to protest. 'No, we must. We feel safer if we carry it. I'll carry your bag. Poppie is going to take off the cloth and lead you into the house. Please co-operate with us – keep looking at the ground. Right. We go in now.'

I glimpsed the twin towers of the power station, quite small in the distance as I got out. We must be in a southerly township, I thought. Scattered images were frozen into my memory – a rusty gate, a short path, clumps of grass, a rosebush – as we entered the house, one of a row of semi-detached cottages that was completely indistinguishable from any other black suburb. Maybe Mannenberg or Hanover Park?

Inside, I was relieved to find the familiar form of Ferdie welcoming us with an expressionless face. I was led into the back room. 'This is Mkonto,' said Ferdie. The young man on the bed greeted me with a wave of his arm – his left one. The right upper arm was bound up with a bandage. He was very young, with the beginnings of a beard. The sweat stood out on his face. He looked ill and toxic. I began taking off the bandages. An almost familiar smell filled the room – it was some common bacterial growth but I couldn't identify it. Mkonto's upper arm had a terrible wound. The humerus was smashed and the two fragments of bone were mobile. He groaned as I moved the lower fragment with the rest of the arm attached. The whole wound was covered with foul-smelling yellow pus.

I willed myself to be calm and methodical but my own feelings of inadequacy kept welling up. I had lurked around the accident unit at Groote Schuur a few months ago, so I had a rough idea what should be done. I called for a bench to rest his arm on and then got him to move his fingers. He could move all his fingers and felt me prick them with a pin. So far so good, I told him, all your nerves are intact. I could tell my four watchers were impressed. I kept them on the hop, fetching boards and hot water, adjusting lights. I was going to attempt a brachial block so that I could scrabble around the wound unhindered. I drew up

10cc of lignocaine into a syringe and, after feeling around his shoulder a bit, pushed the needle in to the hilt. 'Ouch,' he cried.

'Sorry, sorry, haven't you guys a bullet or something for him to bite on?' The other man who had been the passenger in the car groped in his pocket and then realized it was a joke. I drew back the plunger on the syringe and, horror of horrors, got bright red blood back. 'Fuck it, I've hit the subclavian artery.' I pulled out the needle and got Poppie to press a piece of bandage on to the spot. What to do now? I had obviously gone in too medially. The block should be abandoned now, strictly speaking. But it was essential. I didn't have the facilities, or the know-how, to give him a general anaesthetic.

After five minutes and no obvious haematoma appearing on his neck, I tried again, more laterally this time. 'Do you feel anything in your fingertips?'

He nodded. 'It prickles,' he said. Great! At least I was in the right place. Now 5cc or 10? I gave 10 just to be safe, though I had no idea of the correct dose. I should have looked it up this afternoon, I told myself.

'We have to wait 15 minutes to see if it works,' I told the assembled multitude. 'How old is the injury?'

'Five days now,' said Ferdie.

'A bullet?' I asked craftily. He nodded.

I showed them how to prepare the vials of penicillin and streptomycin I had brought, when to give them, and where. I went through my tool box, trying to seem competent. I was feeling happier now that the whole business had begun. But what did I do if the block didn't work?

In fact, it worked beautifully. After 10 minutes Mkonto had no sensation in his arm at all. I cleaned his arm as well as I could, then put the sterile green drapes on the board and covered the limb until only the wound was visible. I scrubbed my hands thoroughly and drew on some plastic gloves. The room was growing oppressively hot, so I decided not to wear a sterile gown, although I had one in my bag. I got Poppie to open the cut-down pack and put some hibitane in the receiver inside it. I cleaned the pus off the wound, then snipped away the flesh that was obviously necrotic and of no use. Now and then I came across some stray bits of metal which I plucked out. The operating field became more and more bloody as clots were dislodged from healthy tissues. I cursed myself for not bringing more swabs. Mkonto kept his spirits up during the whole procedure, chatting away to others who brought him tea and medicinal tots of brandy.

I was not sure of what to do with the bone fragments that were uncovered as I delved deeper into his arm. Eventually, I decided to remove the completely loose ones but leave any that still had flesh attached. I was just beginning to glimpse green towel through the wound, indicating that I had gone through to the other side, when suddenly the whole area filled with blood. I swabbed it away. It refilled. Oh Christ, I thought, is this how the world ends – with my first real patient bleeding to death in front of my eyes? I began to panic, thrusting my hand into the bloody mush to try and find the bleeder by touch. It was no use. The blood was seeping on to the floor now, watched in fascinated horror by Mkonto and the rest. 'Here you,' I screamed at the driver, 'grab his arm here! Now squeeze. Hard as you can.' With the flow of blood stopped, I swabbed the wound clean and tried to find the bleeder. No way. 'Relax a little.' I watched the rush of blood appear from underneath a hitherto undisturbed muscle belly. 'Squeeze again.' I separated the muscle from the surrounding fibres and lifted it. Underneath was what looked like an awfully big, severed blood vessel. I tied it off, my hands shaking so that I could hardly finish the knots. 'Okay, relax,' I told the driver. I looked up at him. His face was sweating as well from the strain. The field stayed relatively dry. I hoped that the vessel wasn't the main blood supply to his arm. No, probably not – it must have been severed by the bullet and his arm hadn't fallen off yet, so there must be a good collateral blood supply to the remainder of the limb.

Everyone began talking at once. The driver clapped me on the back – 'Well done,' he said with his WASPish accent.

Mkonto wasn't looking so flash though. He was pale and weak. 'Give him some more to drink,' I ordered.

I decided to call it a day. The wound was looking fairly fresh – which was to say it seemed to be bleeding slowly from everywhere at the same time. I stuck a drain through his arm and wrapped it up fairly tight, hoping he wouldn't slowly ex-sanguinate in the next hours. Then I taped his arm across his chest, ending with his right hand near his left shoulder. 'It'll have to stay like that for at least six weeks,' I told Mkonto. He nodded. 'It should eventually unite all right but it might take quite a bit longer. I'd like to come back in two days to take the drain out and re-dress the wound. You'll need some more penicillin and streptomycin anyway. Is that . . . permissible?' I asked the whole company. But it was Mkonto who answered with surprising authority.

'We will discuss it when you have gone. We would rather you, and us, didn't have the risk of meeting again. Perhaps we could pick up the medicines from you? We'll see.'

'Well, anyway I'd like to stay until the anaesthetic wears off. It should be in an hour or two.' I was suddenly loathe to leave them. After the ordeal of the past few minutes, I felt very close to the others. I only hoped they felt the same about me.

'No,' said Ferdie firmly. 'We go now before it gets too late for law-abiding people to be awake.'

We rushed out in much the same formation as we went in. 'Don't forget your promise,' I reminded Ferdie as he bound up my eyes.

'Don't you forget to keep your mouth shut about all this,' he replied. He restored my pistol to its holster. I lay down on the floor feeling suddenly exhausted. It was almost midnight when they dropped me off in Claremont at my car.

'We'll be in touch,' said Ferdie shortly, and they drove off, leaving me alone with the glories and the terrors of my first operation.

Two days later the whole rendezvous business was repeated, this time, if anything, with even greater stress on security, to make sure I wasn't leading anybody to them.

I found Mkonto sitting up and looking much better. I gave him some doloxene and valium (the strongest analgesia I had been able to rip off) and then unwrapped the wound gingerly, knowing that every slight jar would be pure agony for him. I was fairly pleased with my handiwork. The wound looked clean and healthy, though there was still a huge gaping mouth in his arm through which the bone could be seen quite clearly. Mkonto gave a piercing scream as I pulled the drain out and fainted away for a few seconds. I re-dressed his arm and prepared to go. I left instructions for Poppie to dress it again in one week and thereafter on alternate days. I left two weeks' supply of pen and strep but told them to use their own discretion about how long they continued the treatment (Mkonto was already complaining about the painful six-hourly intramuscular injections).

'Thank you very much,' said Mkonto as I said goodbye to him. It occurred to me that this was the first gesture of gratitude I had received from any of them. It was quite understandable in a way. They supposed I wasn't doing it for him but for the cause (whatever that was exactly). Meanwhile I was actually doing it for myself.

I bent low over Mkonto, quite a handsome boy really, and whispered in his ear, 'I bank at Nedbank. Why don't you give them the works some time.' He laughed and wagged his finger at me conspiratorially.

'Ferdie . . .' I began.

'I know, I know,' he said as we drove back. 'Just be patient, that's all.'

I was lying on my bed staring at the ceiling and daydreaming of Van Wyk when I suddenly remembered that tonight was the night of my date with Martin. I picked up the phone to call him, thinking I would claim sudden illness, and then replaced the receiver without dialling. I liked Martin, even if I no longer desired him. Well, I thought, who knows what will happen with Van Wyk? I had never really thought of the future with him.

I dressed rapidly in my smartest clothes, a twin set with a white blouse. Too posh, I thought, gazing at my flushed reflection in the mirror. I pulled on a pair of jeans. Too sloppy – and too tight, as I battled with the zip. The indecision gave me a fresh resolve and I dialled Martin this time. No reply.

Back to the wardrobe. I knew I was being absurd. I did not have many clothes, and Martin had certainly seen me wear all of them in the past five years. I tried on a pair of slacks and a big round-necked jersey. The trousers were too short. I'd have to go back to the twin set.

The doorbell rang. I had a ghastly premonition that it was Kaplan again. I pulled on my boots for confidence and flung the door open aggressively.

'Hi, Carol! This is Cousin Benjie and Sheila.'

'Hi!' 'Hi!' 'Hi!' 'Hi!'

I bowed slightly with each greeting, feeling as though we were embarking on some obscure tribal ritual. Martin looked dashing in a blazer and trousers; Cousin Benjie, perfect in a three-piece suit and tie; while Sheila was simply stunning in a silk dress that contrived to be off both shoulders at once.

I ushered them into my tiny flat.

'Sorry about all these clothes lying about. I couldn't make up my mind what to wear. Perhaps I should try and find something smarter anyway . . .?'

'Nah, you look great, Babe,' said Cousin Benjie.

'At least you're not wearing your jeans. I was betting with myself you would be.' Martin smiled gently and squeezed my arm. I had noticed him do that before – the only time he touched me was after saying something unpleasant.

'I believe the food here is fantastic,' said Sheila as we were ushered to our table at 'The Kaapse Tafel'. 'Cape Malay dishes are the speciality.' The restaurant was packed but the atmosphere remained subdued – some would say dead – with the gentlest murmur of conversation lapping at our heels. Naturally there was no trace of 'Cape Malays' present, unless they were in the kitchen. The rest of the crowd, roughly the same age as us, were soberly dressed and spoken.

Cousin Benjie – I had discovered in the car that he was an accountant – opened the first two of the bottles of wine he had brought with him. 'Dad knows this guy who owns the estate in Stellenbosch,' he explained, 'Great stuff.' He filled our glasses and began fooling with Sheila's legs under the table. Martin put his arm across the back of my chair and started talking medicine.

'What do you do?' I asked Sheila hoping to open up the conversation.

'I manage a shoe shop in Sea Point.'

'Really? That's unusual,' I said politely.

'Think so? You should tell her father that. He owns a whole chain.'

'Ouch!' Sheila removed Cousin Benjie's hand from somewhere near her waist, slapped his wrist, and smoothed down her skirt. 'Benjie–eee,' she said reprovingly and flashed me a conspiratorial look.

This was excruciating. I poured myself a second glass of wine.

The waitress arrived to take our order. She was a tall, coloured girl with high cheekbones. I wondered if Rienet looked anything like her. My menu had no prices on it. I sipped on my wine indecisively. I had no wish to make a scene about it.

'Could I please have a menu with prices?' I asked the waitress.

'Don't worry about the cost,' said Cousin Benjie. 'I'm paying.'

This was news to me but did not affect the issue, I felt. 'I'd just like to see the price of things I order,' I said lamely.

'Are you a feminist?' Cousin Benjie pronounced the word with just a hint of distaste. A whole range of vicious responses went through my mind. 'If I don't know the price of the food, how can I judge if I'm getting value in what I order?'

'Do you wear a bra?' Cousin Benjie, I realized, was quite drunk. He looked at my breasts rudely.

'Benjie!' chorused Martin and Sheila.

I gulped some more wine and ordered a Waterblommetie Bredie: a stew with flowers in it.

Over supper, the reason for the celebration emerged. Cousin Benjie had received his green card to go to America. He explained to me at some length how he had managed it. It was, I gathered, a three year saga involving his uncle in Chicago, another cousin who was a surgeon in Detroit, and an expensive lawyer in New York.

'But what'll you do there?' I asked.

'The life in California is fantastic. You can do anything you want. If you're into movies, there are movies; if you're into music . . .' Cousin Benjie was an enthuser.

'No, I mean what work will you do?'

'My uncle has arranged a job in import-export in San Francisco. I'll try and take a few things over with me – local clothes, music, that sort of thing. Look, it'll probably be tough at first, but it'll be great.'

Sheila was going to manage a branch of the shoe-shop chain in Los Angeles and meet up with Cousin Benjie. Even Martin admitted he had written for the American medical entrance exam, the E.C.F.M.G., and was awaiting a reply from a hospital in Atlantic City.

'And you?' he asked.

'I've never given a thought to living in America,' I said. How could I? Van Wyk could not emigrate and still less Rienet. 'I don't want to leave this country, I think.'

'Why not? I believe there are feminists living happily in the States.' Martin grinned at me and dropped his arm off the back of the chair around my shoulders. I waited for him to remove it again but he didn't.

'There's going to be a blood bath in South Africa,' said Cousin Benjie. I leaned forward to grab my wine glass and dislodged Martin's arm.

'I'm going to the toilet,' I mumbled.

I splashed cold water on my face. What, oh what, was I doing in this place? On my way out, I nearly collided with our waitress.

'Excuse me,' I said, 'but do you know Rienet Arendse?'

'What, Madam?' she replied politely.

Was I going crazy? Why was I asking complete strangers about Rienet? I must be drunk.

I returned to the table in time for sweets. The last bottle of wine, the fourth or fifth, had been opened. Cousin Benjie had fallen silent while Sheila and Martin discussed style in California. I could not understand a single reference they made – who are these people and why have I never heard of them, I wondered. Cousin Benjie disappeared to the toilet, and Martin returned his arm to my shoulders.

'I've got a touch of diarrhoea,' I told him. I had to turn my face so that it was very close to his.

'Oh, really? Well I hope you'll be okay to go to a club later on,' he said.

'After all this wine, I don't think any of us will be able to go.'

'No, Cousin Benjie's very keen to go.'

The Gods began to smile on me because Cousin Benjie did not

return after fifteen minutes and Martin discovered him holed up in the gents, too sick from vomiting to walk.

'I don't know why he drinks so much,' confided Sheila to me as we shamefacedly followed Martin half-carrying Cousin Benjie out of the restaurant. 'I've told him a million times to take it easy when we go out.'

I shared Sheila's revulsion. 'At least there wasn't a fist fight,' I said 'We should be grateful for that.'

'Can I come in for coffee?' asked Martin at the door to my flat.

'No, I feel too sick.' I did not think I needed to indulge anyone anymore.

I returned to my position on my bed, addressed the ceiling once more, and, for the first time, began to think that I was lucky to have Van Wyk.

CHAPTER 10

When I finished at medical school the next day, I found a note under my windscreen wiper. 'Meet me at the Adderley Street entrance to the Gardens at eight tonight.'

I drove slowly home to my flat. I knew this was the Big Moment. Rienet would be there, I was certain. I showered and dressed, feeling numb. There was so much I wanted to ask her. What was she trying to do with this bank robbery business? What should I do about Van Wyk? About the Secret Police? About my future?

I touched the laughing Jesus nervously. Our last afternoon together perhaps, little charm and I?

I met Ferdie on time at the start of Government Avenue. We began strolling wordlessly up the avenue. It was just a shade darker than twilight. To our left, the Houses of Parliament were spotlighted in subdued splendour. To our right, we could hear the birds in the Gardens itself. The avenue was deserted.

'Where is she?' I asked hoarsely. I couldn't take the strain much longer.

'Just keep walking,' murmured Ferdie. After a hundred yards or so, I suddenly made out a dark figure sitting on a bench about half-way up the avenue. She was far away, but in the fading light I fancied I could see her face inclined towards us.

I opened my mouth to speak. Just then we passed the middle entrance to the Gardens. There was a scuffle on the gravel, and we both started as a burly figure trotted out to meet us. It was Sergeant Kerneels Cronje of the Security Police.

'And where are you going, Martens?' he said in his gutteral Transvaal Afrikaans.

'You stupid bitch,' hissed Ferdie at me. 'He followed you.'

'Correct. And now, Hotnot, you're going to show me where this Rienet Arendse is. Or I'm going to crush your head in right here.'

Ferdie suddenly darted up the avenue. What a forlorn attempt at escape I thought, as in five steps Cronje overhauled his crippled gait. Cronje tripped him and he fell heavily. As he went down, I could see the figure on the bench rise and waver between retreat and advance. Cronje picked up the small man with one hand and hit him in the face with the other. 'Waar is Rienet, jou verdomde Hotnot. Jou blerrie klonk.' With every phrase he swung his huge fist into Ferdie's face. It made a slapping sound like steak being pounded. I had never seen one human being hit another so hard.

And over his shoulder the slight figure in the gloom suddenly began to run down the gravel path towards us. In that instant I knew Ferdie and Rienet, at least, were doomed unless I stopped Cronje.

'Stop it!' I shrieked. 'Stop it!' I grabbed my gun from its holster in one smooth sweep.

'Stop it or I'll kill you.' Cronje dropped Ferdie like a sack of potatoes and turned towards me.

'You cunt, you blerrie communist English cunt. I knew you were with this scum. I'm going to beat you black and blue, you little cunt.'

'Stop. Stop there or I'll shoot you.' I was almost mesmerized by his chain of curses.

'You blerrie useless student. I'm going to see you hang with your boeties. You terrorist bitch.'

He stood in front of me. With open contempt he pushed my

wavering gun hand aside. 'You useless piece of shit.'

Then Ferdie flung himself on Cronje's back. Cronje let go of me as Ferdie clamped one arm round his neck. Bellowing like an enraged elephant, Cronje flung him off and as he turned back to me I got hit by a spurt of blood right between my eyes. I brushed it away and saw Cronje sink to his knees, his neck a gaping wound, his face almost covered by twin fountains of blood from his bilaterally severed carotid arteries. He scrambled blindly in his jacket for his weapon.

I watched Ferdie rise and coldly kick him above the elbow with his raised steel boot. I heard the bone snap and Cronje rolled over on to his side. His whole head was covered in blood, which continued spurting from his neck. He seemed to take an age of thrashing and gasping to die. At last he wiped one eye clean with his good hand, fixed it on me and gurgled 'Bits!' Then he lay quiet.

Ferdie wiped the long blade of his knife on the dead man's jacket. Far away in the dark, I could see Rienet slowly sitting down again on the bench. Professional to the last. Ferdie pocketed Cronje's huge revolver and wallet.

I could taste blood in my mouth. I opened it and found I'd bitten through two knuckles. My blouse was covered in Cronje's blood. Ferdie stood up slowly. His face was swollen and broken.

'Keep away from me, Ferdie. I've still got my gun.'

'Which you don't use. Relax, Carol, I've got no quarrel with you.'

'But I saw you. I saw you kill him. You can't let me go now.'

'With a bit of help from you, remember? We killed him together. And it's probably the best job you've ever done. He was a vuile, filth. Listen to me. You go back to the police. You tell them almost everything just as it happened. You were trying to find Rienet. This pig followed you, jumped us, and I killed him. Say nothing about Mkonto; say nothing about drawing your gun. Say I ran away after killing him. They'll probably be suspicious, but the most they'll do is hold you for a few days. So long as we're free, they have no proof that you're connected with us. Go now. Just walk slowly to give us a chance to get away.' He turned and limped off rapidly.

'Tell Rienet I'm sorry.' I called after him. He made no reply.

CHAPTER 11

In the event, it all unfolded pretty much as Ferdie had prophesied. When I finally found a policeman, I had no trouble producing a fairly convincing display of hysterics. In fact, the problem was in stopping once I started.

I was detained by the secret police for three days and interrogated morning and afternoon, usually by a dapper little Nazi called Swanepoel. I was loud in blaming the dead Cronje as a bungler – if he hadn't interrupted us, I would have made contact with Rienet and delivered her into Kaplan's hands.

The details of the killing were gone over countless times. I found myself embroidering the basic story more and more with each recounting. The brutality of Ferdie, how he kicked Cronje when he was down, how he threatened me with the knife, but how I managed to escape because I could run faster; all these became mini-epics by the third day.

My reasons for finding Rienet were examined. I tried to stick to the basic truth, so as not to get confused. I told them of her mother and the charm; of my growing fascination with her; and how finally Kaplan and Cronje had pressured me into trying to find her for their own reasons.

Inevitably my own political stance was brought to light. I had decided to adopt the guise of a flabby liberal Progressive Reform Capitulation groupie. It was quite easy really. Enough of my friends and acquaintances were similar crusaders. I just had to prattle earnestly about Peaceful Change (with the accent on 'peace' rather than 'change') before it was *too late*. I could confidently espouse the cause of free enterprise (I had cleared out my room of all Marxist literature afer my first meeting with Kaplan).

What do you think of the ANC? Well if I was black perhaps I'd think differently, and I suppose one can understand blah blah blah, avoid violence at all costs, and so on. I think I carried off that particular charade quite well. My background of two arrests during student demonstrations a couple of years back helped establish my credentials as one with her feet firmly planted in the realm of petit bourgeois politics. The only clue the interrogators had to my true affiliations was my relationship with Van Wyk.

'Tell me, this coloured, Ernest Van Wyk, did he help you look for Rienet?'

'No. Although I first meet him when I tried to trace her at his school.'

'You've known him long?'

'Just a few months.'

'Were you sleeping together?'

'No, we are just friends, good friends.'

'You know, we've had you under surveillance for some time. On' – rustle rustle – '7 October you were observed to enter his house in Steenberg and left only at . . . two a.m.'

'We were talking.'

'And on 11 October, as you drove off, he was observed to put his arm around you.'

'We're friends.'

'And you mean to tell me Ernest never tried to help you find Rienet? In spite of the fact that they were lovers no more than a year ago?'

'I beg your pardon?'

'Don't play stupid with me, Miss Cummings! We know conclusively that Ernest and this Rienet had an affair lasting almost six months in 1972.'

'. . . I never knew.'

'That sounds unlikely. Why should he hide it from you?'

'We . . . never spoke about our sex lives.'

'Did you know that Ernest was a Trotskyite?'

'No. Well, that is, Mr Kaplan mentioned it to me. I didn't know before then. We never discussed politics.'

'Let's see, you never had sex, never spoke about sex, politics or Rienet Arendse. Just exactly what did you do all the time you were together?'

That was the worst session of the three days. Swanepoel meticulously explored every cul de sac I pointed us at before returning to the main road. We spoke at length about cricket (I had mentioned that Van Wyk and I often discussed it); Trotsky; inter-racial sex; why I thought Van Wyk had never talked about Rienet; how he felt about me; and several other little topics that I can't even remember. I returned to my cell feeling dispirited. It was true that they couldn't fault me on the Rienet-Cronje business, but they were tearing my other cover stories to pieces. How long would this go on, I wondered. Weeks? Months? Until they 'broke' me?

There had been none of the violence for which the Secret Police were so infamous. But, after all, I was a white princess who was apparently being completely co-operative.

That evening Kaplan visited me in my cell.

'I've read the investigating officer's reports,' he began brusquely.

'When can I go home?' I didn't have to feign weariness.

'I believe you are more involved in Rienet Arendse and the killing of Sergeant Cronje than you have let on. But the man in charge of the investigation accepts your story at face value. We are both agreed that you are probably of little help at the moment in tracing Arendse and Martens. That is unfortunate. I, we, will have to use other initiatives. I say only this to you: we will be watching you from time to time; just give us cause to suspect, just suspect, that you are dabbling in terrorism or communism again, and you will not see the light of day for a very long time. You can go now.'

I went.

Chocolate was at a headmasters' convention in Port Elizabeth. he would be back only the following Monday – the day I began exams. He, too, I learnt later, had been pulled in by the Secret Police, but was released the same afternoon. Luckily he clung to the same line as I had – both about myself and Rienet. Only he admitted we slept together (which earned him a few clouts around the ear) – but then this probably added a tinge of veracity to both our stories.

On impulse I visited his landlady, Tannie Marie.

'Did you know Rienet Arendse?' I asked her.

She looked a bit embarrassed. 'Ja, she was Ernest's girlfriend before you – a long time ago, last year I think it was. There have been only two girls since Ernest moved in with me. Only two serious ones, you and Rienet.'

'Have you heard about her in another way, since she broke up with, um, Ernest?' She looked decidedly uncomfortable now. She bent close to me and whispered, 'People say she fights the Boere.'

Well, that explained where Amien Sonday and Mrs Isaacs got these fantastic stories about her. She was fighting the Boere, and they had tried to keep me from her. In the case of Sonday, he had just tried a bit harder. I suddenly realized that I hadn't thought of revenge on Sonday for a long time. It no longer seemed to be necessary, I thought.

The first day of exams went well. For the only section I would normally have struggled in, respiratory physiology, I contrived to sit behind Martin. He seemed pretty confident in most of his answers, so I supposed I could be as well.

Later, the 'boys' and I had our obligatory cup of tea in order to preside as usual (I thought) over the post mortem of the day's examinations. Instead, I found that I was the subject of the discussion.

'So, uh, tell me, Carol,' began Raymond, 'what really happened between you and that cop?' There had been a short piece in the newspapers reporting Cronje's death and also that an 'eyewitness and female medical student' were being detained for questioning. It also, unfortunately, mentioned me by name.

'Did it have anything to do with, whatsername, Rienet?'

For an instant I felt tempted to tell them the whole complex story. It seemed so long ago since it had begun with a tea-time bullshit session. But the impulse passed and with it, too, passed the remains of any closeness that existed between myself and the three of them.

'Ag, no, nothing,' I evaded. 'It's too long a story to tell.' I steered the conversation round to our three-month elective periods which began the following week. I was attached to Middlesex Hospital in London – in fact, all four of us were going overseas – no flies on us, or rather our parents. I was beginning to get a bit excited about the trip. My initial sense of betrayal by Chocolate had given way to a numb bewilderment which made it much easier to look forward to my coming holiday. Chocolate is a turd, I kept on thinking, and in one week I'd be 5,000 miles away. Or was it 8,000?

Van Wyk was waiting outside my flat in his Kombi. I was shocked at the involuntary tummy flutter as I clambered in beside him. He started the engine and drove off, a neat trick so that he didn't have to look at me.

'You okay?'

I nodded, too overcome with yearning to speak.

'What actually happened between you and that pig?' Oh, damn him.

'Chocolate, how could you, how could you, how could you?'

My anger at my whining weakness was the last straw. I broke down and cried. Van Wyk said nothing for a long time, pretending to concentrate on driving while I snuffled in the background. Then at last he spoke.

'Rienet was the most important thing that had ever happened to me. We were lovers for six months before we, before she, decided that she didn't want to see me anymore. When I look back on the six months, they seem very happy, though I didn't realize it at the time. We fought a lot, mostly about politics. I still regard her as essentially an opportunist, albeit of great ability, but we learnt a lot, too – me more than her. When she left I was heartbroken, desolate. I thought I would never recover. And in fact I didn't, not until a young white medical student walked into my office three months ago.

'The likeness between Rienet and the student was almost uncanny – the same verve, the same urgency about them, even the same mannerisms. After a while I couldn't tell which gestures were originally hers and which Rienet's. They had blurred in my mind. The irony of it shrieked at me every day – here was this girl searching for Rienet yet, to me, becoming more like her with every day that passed.

'What could I do? I knew I had to see you again after our first meeting. But I also knew that a confrontation between you and Rienet could be catastrophic for her – for all three of us probably. So I baited you with half-clues, with hints of people who knew Rienet only slightly. And when it seemed that I had you, that you slept with me for my own sake, not necessarily to get closer to her, then I tried to shut off your search. But fate was on your side. Who could have dreamt that Ferdie Martens would become her lieutenant? That you would pursue him so persistently? That you would meet, or nearly meet her, when half the police force in the town had failed?

'What could I do? I had to keep on seeing you; I couldn't tell you of my previous relationship with her 'cause you would have demanded to be put in touch with people closer to her. All I could manage was to try to persuade you to give up the search. But I failed – as I would have failed if I'd try to dissuade her from something she was set on.

'So here I am now. I'm in love with you – or her – or both of you – or some curious amalgam of the two. But I am in love – and you are all I have left.' He seemed to want to say more, but the last sentences weighed heavily on both of us and they were unretractable, unalterable. I suppose it's an ego boost when someone says they love you – but it's all downhill when they go on to say they're not sure if it's somebody else, or you because you remind them of somebody else.

'Oh, Chocolate. You could have lied to me about anything and it wouldn't have mattered all that much. But about Rienet? You know how important it was, is, to me. She was the one thing I wanted most. You deceived me about her not because you feared for her safety but because you didn't want me to discover your affair. You were too scared to end this Rienet-Carol personality infusion in your head. You were actually enjoying fantasizing that I was her. She . . .'

'No, that's an over-simplification. I didn't fantasize that you were her – in many ways you *are* her. Haven't you ever wondered why Ferdie didn't put a knife through your neck? He must see it, too . . .'

We drove on in silence for a time.

'Anyways,' he continued, 'I'm sorry for lying, but I felt I could do nothing else. I still want to see you, very much. And I have a plan, a political project we can both work on. I think it's a good one.'

'Well, I dunno. I can't think at the moment what to do. But, conveniently for a poor decider like me, I've got exams all this week and I'm leaving early next for the UK. So if I wanted to see you – I wouldn't have a chance for the next three months. I'd like that time to think about the whole affair.

You probably could do with the contemplative time too.'

He nodded as he turned the car for home. 'I'll miss you,' he said.

'I'll miss you, too,' I replied with a sigh, knowing it to be true.

He kissed me tenderly outside my flat and I climbed out hurriedly, feeling tearful again.

'I love you,' he said as I pressed the door closed. I can picture his face now – little boy-earnest Ernest, eyebrows raised, head cocked, misty-eyed.

I never saw him again.

CHAPTER 12

Two days later, I was just getting out my car at lunchtime, having returned from the morning's boring exam. Feelings of weltschmertz were common for me before exams, but I'd never experienced them during the actual examination week before. I was thinking (again) about dropping out of medicine. How could I stand another year of this purgatory?

Just then, a wizened black lady shambled up to me. 'Merrem, have you got 20 cents for bus fares?' I've long ago understood my feelings towards beggars – I hate them. No matter which response one gives them, a kick in the arse or a pat on the head, the relationship is the same – you hate each other. 'No, I'm sorry, I won't,' I replied, not too pleasantly.

The old crone rambled on about her 97 children and no husband as I picked up my books. Then, still speaking in the same monotonous undertone, she grabbed my sleeve. 'Rienet wants to see you.'

'What?'

'Rienet wants to see you in the same place you saw her last. Wait for her there. You must go now.'

I pushed a 50 cent coin at her and scrambled back in the car.

It was almost two o'clock when I arrived at Government Avenue. The contrast with the last time I had been there was sharp: it was a bright, hot day, and the Avenue was crowded with office workers strolling around. I looked for the place where

Cronje had died, expecting to see a blood stain of some description, but there was none; I couldn't even be sure of the spot.

I ambled up the Avenue, looking for familar faces or Rienet-like forms. There were none. I remembered my instructions to wait and selected a bench, roughly where I had seen Reinet before. It was dappled by the sun and the leaves of an overhanging tree. I opened my newspaper, feeling strangely calm. The chief of the Secret Police had vowed to capture and punish the dastardly group of 'Urban Terrorists' who had been raiding banks. At the same time he appealed for information leading to their capture and hinted at a reward.

I turned the page.

Someone eased on to the bench beside me.

'Hello, Carol,' she said.

Rienet was just as I'd imagined her – yet different. She was quite short, shorter than I even, with very smooth, muscular arms. Her hair was tucked behind her ears. She wore newish blue jeans and a military style blouse – an unremarkable affectation, everyone was wearing them that year. To my surprise her accent was strongly Cape Coloured.

I was suddenly awkward and tongue-tied. 'I've been looking for you,' I said irrelevantly.

'I noticed,' she said with a smile. 'It's good to meet after all this time. You did a good job on Mkonto. He's feeling fine, but his arm's still a bit sore. We've managed to get him away from the Cape – and Ferdie, too. It was quite an effort – one with a game leg and one with a game arm. Did the vuiles treat you all right?'

'Not too bad. I'm sorry about the other night.'

'No, it wasn't your fault entirely. We should have been more careful to make sure you weren't followed. And it was about time that Ferdie went underground. We'd been delaying it because he's so noticeable it would be difficult for him to work in the open again. So there was no harm done really. You learn from your mistakes – if you survive them.'

She had her mother's eyes, deep and green and set wide apart. Up close there was a rash of freckles across the dark skin of her nose and cheeks.

'Do you have a big . . . group?' I asked.

'Getting bigger all the time.' She smiled a lot. 'We've got funds now, too – that'll make a difference.'

'You heard about me and Amien Sonday? Is he part of the group?'

'No, he knows nothing of us. But he'd heard of us. The vuiles and their spies are our biggest publicity agents – moving among the people in the townships and asking if they know where we are. So Amien was just doing what he thought was best for me. I know it must have been a terrible experience, but you mustn't be too hard on him. He overreacted, but at least he acted in the right direction.'

We were silent for a while. How strange, I thought, to meet the object of my obsession after all this time.

'What of you, Rienet? Don't you want children? A man? Security and all that bourgeois trash?'

'How is Ernest?' It was as if she read my mind.

'He's . . . well. He never told me you were lovers. The first I heard of it was from the Secret Police.'

She nodded and smiled. 'He's a professional, too. A professional conspirator.' I bristled. How dare she sneer at my lover – my ex-lover – even if he was hers, too?

'You've got to have a revolutionary ideology before you can have a revolution,' I retorted primly.

Rienet smiled affectionately and covered my hand with her own. It was strong and warm. I felt myself respond almost sexually to her.

'You have to tread between theory and action. I think Ernest is too far into theory; he thinks I'm too much into action – an opportunist he calls me. You've got to be reassessing your position all the time or else you can't tell where you're going.'

I nodded. I turned my hand over and clasped hers. 'I think he's doing that at the moment – having a big reassessment, I mean. I was very hurt that he never told me he had had an affair with you. He knew how much it meant to me.'

'But he had loyalties to me as well as you, surely, Carol? Anyway, we've met now and so it doesn't matter. He's a very fine person – a great mind. Also, he's very good in bed.' We tittered away like schoolgirls.

'Do you have anybody at the moment?' I asked. 'What about Ferdie?'

'No, Ferdie and I are just good comrades.' Rienet's eyes light up when she smiles. 'Ag, no, you know I'm too busy to have a serious relationship at the moment. I take a bit of piel now and then, when I feel I need it.' I was shocked at her crudity.

'You're shocked,' she said solemnly.

'No, no,' I insisted. 'Well . . . yes. It seems a very . . . mechanical attitude.'

'Perhaps. But I'm more efficient when I'm not frustrated. And I can't afford to get involved with anyone now – it would be too distracting.'

'It must be difficult to lead your group. The males must resent it a bit – it's inevitable surely.'

'I'm not the leader, strictly speaking. I'm more a kind of . . . elder statesman.' She laughed huskily. 'But you're right. You've got to be strong with these men or they'll have you making tea and sandwiches while they decide what's to be done. I suppose that's true even if you aren't a revolutionary.'

'It's so strange,' I said. 'I've longed to meet you for so long now. I wanted to ask you all these questions. I suppose in a way you've become a comic-book figure for me – a dare-devil superwoman flying through the air holding up banks and blowing up fascist institutions. I mean, you're a hard act to follow: what do I do now with my life? Medicine seems so pointless by comparison . . .'

Rienet was silent for a long time.

'Carol,' she began slowly, 'you must understand that what we do is not as romantic, or even as correct, as you think. Again, I'll have to tell you things that I shouldn't. The group formed at first around me, and I imposed my vision of what needed to be done. I was so angry, so impatient that I just wanted to smash whatever was in the way. But, as new comrades joined us, particularly Mkonto, they began to ask what sort of new society we were struggling for. I'd never really considered this question – I thought it was enough to attempt to disorganize the state. But the South African state is complex and very powerful. Look, one can see in the next few years black rule coming to Mozambique, Angola, Rhodesia and South West Africa, but that's not going to change things very much. These states will still be controlled from Pretoria to some extent – not by force, but by economic might. I used to think that if we could beat the South African police and army, we could overthrow the State. I admit that was too simple. If one looks forward to real change in this country, only the workers can do it – and by change I mean changing the system of exploitation, not just the people in charge.

'But look at the working class at the moment. They can't even sustain a trade union movement, never mind build a revolution. What they need is not bank robbers, but organization. We've got the money we need. Now we plan to go back to real grass roots work . . .'

'You sound just like Van Wyk now,' I said.

'Only in theory. Don't tell him what I've been saying. He would only crow,' she laughed. 'Carol, finish your degree. The struggle proceeds in many strange ways. Don't be like me – like I was: impatient. We will win in the end, but it might take twenty years. There are many things for a progressive doctor to do in this country.'

107

We were silent a while.

'I have to go soon,' she said.

'Will I see you again?' It suddenly seemed just as important to meet her again as it had before I had spoken to her.

'I'm sure – but not for a long time probably. You must never try to contact me again. Or any of the others. You've no idea how much we've talked over your doings and rushing around. In fact, there was a strong element that thought you should be . . . eliminated, for safety's sake. Think how close Ferdie and I came to catastrophe the other night. We should never have been placed in that position – not that I'm blaming you, but you see the others had a point when they said you were a danger. And when we asked you to help Mkonto – well, we were all up half the night arguing about it. He was getting sicker so fast that in the end we felt we had to take the chance. Actually, it was Ferdie who was dead against anything being done to you.'

'He was?' I was surprised.

'Ja,' she was laughing. 'He said you were just like me. Here come my friends,' she said suddenly. Ambling along towards us, I saw the driver from the other night and another young black I didn't know. They walked loose-hipped and casual, but were gazing up at the top end of the Avenue, probably checking out the escape route one more time.

'Before you go – here,' I showed Rienet the laughing Jesus round my neck.

'Oh that's it. You know I don't remember it at all. I hardly remember my mother, let alone that charm.' She fingered it reflectively. 'It's got a bit of gold on it – not worth much, though. Anyway, we don't need the money now. You keep it for a while, Carol. When we meet again you can give it to me. Oh, we'll bump into each other at, say, the Mount Nelson Hotel in about five years' time, and you'll say, very cool, "I believe this is yours" and I'll say, "Yes, thank you for keeping it for me" . . .'

'Yes, except I'll be there to have a drink, and you'll be there to blow it up.' We laughed loudly as the two drew abreast of us. Then suddenly she clasped me to her in a powerful bear hug and kissed my cheek. She jumped up and linked arms with the two men, and they walked away, a little more rapidly than before.

I watched them disappear into the crowd surging up the Avenue. I sank back on the bench unable to catch my breath, feeling tearful but incapable of crying.

It was only later that night that I remembered when I had felt that way before. It was on my sixteenth birthday, just after being kissed for the first time. I thought then, as I had at sixteen, that one could still die of love.

But I didn't.

CHAPTER 13

My three months in London were personally rather uneventful. But back home in South Africa, once I left the scene, the play had picked up markedly.

In November-December there was a series of strikes in Cape Town which spread to the Eastern Cape. Mainly industrial and building trades were involved, where both defeats and victories were registered. A call for a city-wide general strike was a resounding flop. The demands were mainly economist, but here and there were political objectives – such as the repeal of the pass laws and, in one case, that the factory be run by a worker-management committee, or so it was reported in the London papers.

Van Wyk and his Trot friends finally got off their collective behinds and produced a flurry of agitational pamphlets to selected factories. As Kaplan had predicted, the entire group was picked up with ridiculous ease and brought to an early trial under the Terrorism Act. Unexpected hero of the proceedings was fat-arsed Andrew, who shed his cape of benignity as he was being arrested, battered one Secret Policeman to death with his bare hands, then took his revolver and mortally wounded his colleague who was waiting downstairs. He then dramatically kissed his wife and kids goodbye and made off in the unmarked police car, heading apparently for the Botswanan border some 1,000 miles away. Who knows where he got the petrol from during his night-long dash, but when he was finally ambushed just after dawn the next day, he was less than a hundred miles from the border. A helicopter load of 'crack' anti-terror policemen blasted him and his car to kingdom come just outside Vryburg, a small town in the Northern Cape.

The others, including Van Wyk, stood trial just before Christmas. The evidence consisted of the printing press, plus samples of all the pamphlets found in a garage rented to one of the thirteen. Thrown in were Andrew's behaviour and a full confession by one of the defendants who showed up in court with such a badly smashed jaw he had to write notes to his lawyer (whom he hadn't met before) telling him that he was with-drawing it. The judge decided to accept the confession anyway, quoting some mumbo-jumbo legal precedent.

Faced with all this, the Trots changed their plea to guilty and were duly found so. Van Wyk was the first to make his statement from the dock. A trashy British Trotskyite paper reprinted it in full, while the *Guardian* (who heartwarmingly described him as 'boyishly handsome' and a 'compelling orator') published generous excerpts. I still have it with me. It is a marvel of clear, concise Marxist analysis and prophecy, completely free of backbiting or ultra-left cant. In it, Van Wyk briefly analyses the contending classes in the struggle, stresses his faith in a Socialist system founded by a dictatorship of the proletariat, and concludes with a detailed defence of revolutionary violence.

The speech was immediately banned from publication inside South Africa but has since become a minor underground classic. It ends with the words:

'Your worship, when Ghandi faced a British judge, he told him "you have only two choices: give me the severest sentence possible under the law or resign and join my protest". I know you have only one choice – to punish me as ruthlessly as befits a class enemy. For you, at once a symbol, and a partaker in the spoils of the ruling class, can show no mercy to the revolutionary working class and its supporters. I can expect no gesture except

111

one of bitterness and hatred. I return in kind to you and all you stand for: I piss on you.'

Apparently, he already had his pants down when the guards dragged him from the court. He received 14 years under the Terrorism Act, plus one year for contempt of court.

In a month when I was already reeling with grief and shock, December brought me another trauma. According to SA police sources, a bomb factory in Johannesburg blew itself to pieces. Inside, three charred bodies were found, including one Rienet Arendse.

I passed almost into a state of catatonia. I didn't leave my digs for four days, eating only baked beans. Eventually I emerged and compulsively bought and borrowed South African news-papers in an effort to find out more details. The Johannesburg *Sunday Times* did a long feature article on Rienet, tracing her early years, her political growth and her 'terrorist' career. They even interviewed Didee. Most of it was apocryphal, I'd say – large chunks of their biography I knew to be untrue, and several of their reported escapades (such as executing an insubordinate comrade, and being trained in Kiev) were just too far-fetched.

One encouraging detail was in the description of the three bodies. Burnt beyond recognition, according to the *Sunday Times*, Rienet's large, almost six-foot frame was 'readily identi-fiable'. How? – Rienet – six foot? I began to feel a little better. The line of the *Sunday Times* was 'look how the Government's evil race policies drive talented people into the arms of violence and terrorism.'

The Rienet bandwagon was leapt on by the English-language dailies. Other anecdotal snippets about her were dredged up; even one, finally, linking her to the imprisoned Trotskyite group via the enigmatic Van Wyk. The London *Observer* ran an article on her too, summarizing the growing myth which had sprung up overnight. Entitled 'New Breed of Foe for White South,' the story accentuated Rienet's alleged bravery and verve.

Then, a few days later, something happened to clinch the case in my mind for her survival. Speaking at Loskop Dam to a Raportryer's Congress, the Minister of Police launched a blistering attack on certain newspapers who were trying to make a heroine out of a known murderess and terrorist. He threatened administrative action against these 'certain newspapers' which were trafficking in rumour and half-truths. As an afterthought, he vowed to continue the struggle against Communism and terrorism wherever it reared its ugly head, and so on.

Why, I asked myself, rail against the publicity for a dead martyr – unless the martyr was very much alive and operational? So I returned to South Africa feeling content about Rienet, at least. I have faith, just as she had, that we'll meet again. And, until then, I keep the laughing Jesus around my neck, where he belongs.

POSTSCRIPT

Van Wyk was on Robben Island, so tantalizingly close to Cape Town, just a few miles across Table Bay. The Island has a better record than Alcatraz – only two prisoners in its history are unaccounted for, and they're presumed drowned. So there's no hope of escape.

Tannie Marie visited him after a few months (one of two visits he's permitted each year). She said he's in good spirits but he advised me not to try and see him. But, he said, come the revolution or 14 years and 8 months, whichever is first, Muhammad Ali will be making a comeback – and I'd better be in shape. I cried a lot about that message, too.

I saw Mkonto in a bus once. He grinned at me and raised both arms in the air in a gesture of recovery and victory. We didn't speak.

And so here I am now – six months from graduation. I've tried to put into practice all I learnt from Rienet – and Van Wyk – but that's another story. I live with an artist and three dogs in a cottage in Hout Bay. He is a sculptor and a quiet, gentle person, my lover, who seems to understand when I drive out by myself some evenings to Melkbosstrand, the closest point to the Island, watch the lights on it wink out one by one, and howl like a dog at the moon.